I Am the
Withered Man

NOVELS BY JOHN CREASEY

SEVEN TIMES SEVEN
DANGEROUS JOURNEY
THE WITHERED MAN
I AM THE WITHERED MAN

I Am the Withered Man

John Creasey

David McKay Company, Inc.
Ives Washburn, Inc.
New York

I Am the Withered Man

Originally published under John Creasey's
pen name of Norman Deane

First American Edition, 1973

C

Contents

1

I Receive Information

I watched the car turn into the gateway of my home. It was the middle car of three, and in it sat one man. The first and the last cars each held three black-dressed Storm Troopers; strong, ruthless men, none with weakness in his character, none with a mistaken sense of mercy, or of that 'humanity', in the name of which so many evils have been committed on the Fatherland and so many false accusations levelled against it. I knew those men well; no man or woman entered the grounds of my house, wide spacious grounds high on a hillside overlooking Vienna, not far removed from the sacrosanct castle of Berchtesgarten, unless I knew all that there was to know of him—or unless he was under guard.

Such a man was the solitary passenger in the middle car. I can see him now.

I distrusted him because he was bare-headed, and his hair was dark. I have often been assured by pathologists and others that there are proved cases of men of Aryan and Prussian and Germanic blood having dark hair, but it is not my conviction. I have a hatred of cross-breeding, no matter how far back in the genealogical dossier of my subject. Where blood has been mixed weakness can develop. Yet I knew that Ernst von Stroem was by reputation not only strong and ruthless but thorough; it was he who knew of the existence, on board a troopship going to Norway in the early days of the war, of an English spy; and after obtaining the transhipment of those members of the Gestapo and of the officers in whom he could place full reliance, had the ship torpedoed. There was no single survivor.

7

At that time I was in England.

I had planned for many years the establishment of the new order in England. The Führer himself discussed with me the arrangements, and was graciously pleased to approve of them. It was partly because of this approval that I live: yet at times I wonder if I had not better died for my failure. To those who bring me excuses for failure I have nothing but contempt: I have that same contempt for myself, because I failed to subjugate England.

I returned to the Fatherland for my punishment. It has been whispered that I was not executed because I am physically disabled: I do not believe that. Nor do I believe that the Führer reversed the verdict of the secret trial solely because my defending counsel reminded the Court of his gracious approval of the plans which miscarried. It is and will always remain my belief that the one burning desire in his heart as well as in mine is the triumph of the Fatherland over England. I believe that the Führer considered it possible that an opportunity to use my unusual gifts would occur again and the merited punishment for failure was suspended because of that.

I was retired to my home.

For nearly a year I took no active part in the development of the Third Reich. I watched with disdain the faint-hearted attempts of the Italians to overcome Greece and other nations: I have never liked the Italians; they have been softened by the sun. I watched with increasing hatred the accursed British, led by the thrice-damned Churchill, parry our thrusts and grow stronger. I burned with an increasing desire to work against them, especially to defeat a British man and a British woman. Those two people, virtually unaided, not only wrecked my high hopes, but brought my country to face a long, protracted war of attrition.

Murdoch: Bruce Murdoch and his woman.

I have learned that they are married: I can believe that in the midst of the stress and turmoil of the war they could be happy with each other, yet I know that in them exists a devotion to their Motherland as great as mine to my Fatherland. I have a powerful left hand which has strangled enemies of the Reich; and it aches often to bury itself deep

8

in Murdoch's neck; then in the slim throat of the woman Dell.

I do not hide from the truth: there is no power left to a man who attempts to. My hatred for those two people obsessed me. It obtruded in my dreams; it kept me wakeful and restless at night. It soured my food, it poisoned my wine, it dulled my thoughts.

I have seen men examined by the truncheon and the whip, lashed until they hung dead from the posts which held them, and I pictured Murdoch's blood welling from the cuts, I saw Murdoch's fair hair mingled with blood, I heard Murdoch shrieking, and crying, and moaning, and whispering and dying. I have seen women stripped and beaten and lashed and maltreated and I have imagined the woman Dell, toothless and bloody-mouthed in the picture in my mind, with hair torn from the roots and cheeks gashed, or raddled with acid, with fingers cut to the first and second joints, screaming and raging and pleading.

But those thoughts were not with me when von Stroem came.

My visitors at this time were few. Individuals from the Führer for information that only my retentive memory can supply comprised most of them. Not since I had returned from England had I seen one man of importance.

I had been told by telephone that von Stroem was coming. I had supplemented my memory with information from a dossier which I keep of every man and woman of consequence in the Third Reich. I knew that von Stroem was in favour with Goering and Goebbels, but that the Führer was not at all times sympathetic towards him. I knew that von Stroem had worked for six months in Vichy, contriving to persuade Laval and Bonnet, Badouin and others to do what was wanted.

I did not move from my chair.

My right side is withered: the sickness began during the war of 1914–18, when I was in an aeroplane which crashed, and afterwards I was told that I was fortunate to be alive. Until the birth of the National Socialist regime I cursed the fact that I was not dead, but did not kill myself, confident that one day there would be an opportunity

9

again for serving the Fatherland. The cattle would not always rule.

I cannot use my right leg except when I have injected into it a serum which for short periods makes me physically almost normal, and I do not use this serum except in case of great urgency. By no manner of means could von Stroem's visit be called urgent. I sat in my long-chair, therefore, with my left leg stretched in front of me, and with my stick at my side. I watched the cars disappear, and waited until there was a tap at my door.

'Come in,' I called.

Fritz entered: he is a man of sixty, who has served me well since I can remember. He had about him the air of uncertainty and apprehension which I see so often in servants.

'Your Excellency—it is His Excellency Baron von Stroem.'

'He may enter,' I said.

'Yes, Your Excellency, at once.'

Fritz went out, jerking his white head forward. I had considered the possibility that it had been decided that my period of usefulness was past. I would not have complained, although I would have preferred to hear that from the Leader himself.

von Stroem entered alone. He is tall and upright. His face is young but his eyes are raddled, those of a man who knows too much of wine and women. I admired what I knew of him but my personal feeling was of sharp dislike.

He bowed from the waist: I inclined my head, and said stiffly:

'You understand that I cannot rise.'

'I understand perfectly,' he said, and placed his hat and gloves on my desk. I dislike my desk being sullied by anything that is not mine, but I made no sign. 'I hope, Excellency,' he went on, 'that I have not called on an unfortunate day.' He looked at my leg, and I returned his stare.

'I am perfectly capable of accepting any message,' I said, 'and should it be necessary I can move.'

He smiled: I fancied that there was a sardonic expression in his light blue eyes, and I thought it strange that his eyes should be that colour, since his hair was dark.

'I assure you, Excellency, I meant only a solicitous remark. I know too much of you to doubt your ability to work. I deplore that your services have for so long been denied the Fatherland.'

I detested the fellow for his gloating, and yet he was not a man who would come to gloat but for nothing else.

'Thank you,' I said.

'And I come to bring you the opportunity of further service,' he went on. 'I am faced with a problem which only the most experienced and efficient mind can deal with, and I was compelled to appeal to the Leader for assistance. He graciously asked me to name my choice—and,' added von Stroem gently, 'my choice fell on you, Excellency.'

I felt my heart beating fast: the affliction on my right side makes that at times unavoidable, and in moments of stress I can feel the constriction in my chest and throat. I would have rather taken the opportunity from any other man than Ernst von Stroem, but at his words I could have blessed him, for it gave me back a lease of life.

I said hoarsely, cursing my own emotions:

'I am grateful, Excellency. In what way can I assist?'

'It concerns Vichy,' said von Stroem, and I remembered his reputation for wasting no words. 'You will doubtless be familiar with my efforts there. I have enabled the Fatherland to obtain the use of part of the French Fleet, and some of the French Colonial possessions are now under our control. But they are too few.'

von Stroem was virtually confessing a failure, and had come to me for help! And I had thought that he was gloating over my infirmity! I took my stick, and slowly raised myself. He was watching. I felt the veins in my forehead standing out, and the warmth of sweat on it. I felt the pressure at my heart, and gritted my teeth to withstand it. I thought I must collapse, but succeeded in reachin my feet, although I swayed. I steadied myself, and with the aid of my stick walked to the desk. I have to take one step at a time, steadying myself on my left leg, and then placing the stick firmly ahead of me before dragging my

11

right leg. The stick thuds heavily against the floor. *Thump* —and the pressure goes from one sound leg. A pause, and: *thump!*

I reached my desk chair and lowered myself to it, hanging the stick on a hook specially placed for that purpose.

'I am at your service,' I said.

'I am grateful, Excellency,' said von Stroem. He waited until I was breathing more easily, before saying: 'Until some three months ago the task in Vichy was progressing well. From then on unforseen difficulties arose. There was no apparent reason for them, and many were accidental— or so it seemed. You will recall that Manet, so favourable to the Franco-German accord, died in a car accident. Others, also helpful, died or disappeared. I became aware that someone was deliberately barring my path. I arrested more than three thousand suspected British sympathisers, and many were executed, but the difficulties remained. You will understand my concern, Excellency.'

How well I understood! I nodded.

'It was not until a week ago that I discovered one thing which could explain some measure of the persistence of the sabotage,' said von Stroem. 'I learned that two British agents reputedly in England had in fact flown from England to Spain, but had been wrecked off Cap Finisterre. By thorough investigation I discovered that they had not perished, but had landed in France. Their reputation is such that I had little doubt that they could explain much of my troubles.'

I felt my heart beating so fast that I was choking. I saw two faces looming in front of me; the man with a sardonic smile on his lips, the woman grave-faced but with mocking laughter in her eyes.

von Stroem went on:

'And I know you will understand my belief also when I tell you that the man Murdoch and the woman Dell have been identified from several unimpeachable sources as the agents to whom I refer. Now you will see why I have come to you, my dear Baron.'

2

I Prepare

I was trying to believe what von Stroem told me, yet it seemed an opportunity so remote and so incredible that it must be false. I had to strain my self-control to the uttermost to prevent myself from accusing him of raising my hopes deliberately in order that he might sweep them aside. I have heard of many cruel jokes which he has played, which I do not consider necessary. Cruelty is a word which is often misapplied. There is no cruelty in inflicting physical punishment on recalcitrant prisoners, there is none in maltreating Jews—would one hesitate to kick a dog? If it has a constructive object, if it is the means by which information can be obtained, physical torture should not only be approved, it should be extolled. I have known a thousand cases where the lash of a whip enabled the cause of the Third Reich to be advanced; I will never hesitate to order the severest treatment in such cases.

But it was said that von Stroem perpetrated these hoaxes for his own amusement.

Stroem was looking at me with his eyes narrowed; the window was behind me, and the light was therefore fully on his face: I prefer that position, for then I can see every movement and every expression of my visitors, while they must look at my shadowed face. I thought then that von Stroem should wear glasses.

'How can you be sure of this?' I demanded.

'I do not think, Excellency, that there is any need for me to go into details on that score,' said von Stroem. 'I have with me the details which will I am sure satisfy you. Those two agents are working against me, and are meeting with more success than I would admit to any man but you. And that only because you can understand such set-backs,' he added, in the manner which I was to learn so well. He contrived to put a barb into many of his sentences.

13

'Proceed,' I said. My good left hand was playing with the key of a drawer in my desk.

'I have little more to say,' said von Stroem, 'except that I hope you will lose no time in coming to Vichy.'

I inserted the key in the lock.

'Once I am satisfied of the accuracy of your reports,' I said, 'I will leave here.' I turned the key, and pulled open the drawer. In it were two files. They contained all I knew of Murdoch and Dell.

There were days when I would find my only relief was to take them out and study them, although I knew every minor detail by heart. Murdoch for instance had the smallest of moles on the inside of the cleft in his chin.

I took out the files, and opened them, extracting a book of photographs, enlargements of many taken at various times. They showed both man and woman, full-face and in profile, and from every angle. I selected the full-face of Murdoch, and von Stroem moved round the desk to see.

Murdoch's was a handsome face by normal standards.

It would not have been hard to believe that he was a Scandinavian, even a German. His hair is very fair and crisp, and he likes it to be cut short, particularly at the sides. His grey eyes are exceptionally wide-set. They are, as I know to my cost, deceptive eyes. The peculiarity of them is that the right is faintly narrower at the outer corner than the left—a barely measurable discrepancy, but as plain to me as if he had one blind eye.

His nose, short and very straight, makes his upper lip look shorter than it is. His mouth is wide, and both lips particularly well-shaped. How often I have seen it curve at the corners, even in situations which for Murdoch seemed hopeless. He has a gift of laughter; if I did not hate him so much I would admire him for his courage.

His chin, which is prominent and makes the lower lip appear somewhat full, has a deep cleft. His forehead is broad and high, with the hair growing well back. Murdoch is thirty-five; he might pass anywhere for thirty.

In that photograph he was not smiling, although his eyes appeared to mock me. That quality he has in common with the woman Dell, although her eyes are blue, and her hair

14

dark—plentiful, wavy hair which she grooms excellently. I placed her photograph over Murdoch's.

Both pictures had been coloured: Elsa, who had worked with me for many years, was at one time an art student in Berlin, and she is clever both with painting and retouching photographs. She had worked on these, for she hates the couple as much as I do.

The woman Dell might have been in the room, looking at us.

'That is a beautiful photograph,' said von Stroem.

'She is a beautiful woman,' I admitted. 'If she would realise the duty of a woman is in the home, she might be a splendid example of the sex.' I looked into her round blue eyes, her red lips which are wide and well-shaped; she was smiling, and a glimpse of white teeth showed. Her dark hair was pulled down a little over her forehead.

My right hand found sudden strength, for the photograph began to crumple at one corner; I hardly realised that I was exerting such pressure. I eased it, and replaced the photographs. 'Is there anything you want to know of them?' I asked.

'No more than I can get in Vichy,' said von Stroem. 'I have been to Berchtesgarten. It took longer than I expected, and I must hurry. Baron, there is a matter of considerable importance. The Führer is to visit Vichy. Have you been informed?'

'Who am I to be informed?' I demanded.

'You are now at work, my dear Baron! The Führer, I say, is to visit Vichy. There he is to interview Mondel.'

Mondel had been a Prime Minister of France in the days when that country was swollen with a conceit for itself, instead of its dependence on the Reich. But always he had been sympathetic; he paid lip-service to Daladier, to Chamberlain and Churchill, but I myself had interviewed him, and knew of his real devotion to a totalitarian France. I do not believe in his regard for Germany: he is a Frenchman. But he believes in the methods of our *regime,* and few men would be able to apply those methods so well to France. He owns, amongst many other things of importance, several newspapers which carry considerable weight.

15

One, *Le Dernier Soir,* was suspended during the brief battle of France.

But Mondel had not figured prominently in the discussions between Berlin and Vichy. Laval had ousted him from the position of chief envoy; but Laval, so doing, had lost much popularity amongst his defeated countrymen. Mondel would know better than that, but undoubtedly the French would trust him more than Laval.

'I am not surprised,' I said.

'In three days' time,' said von Stroem, 'Mondel is to print a *verbatim* account of his interview with the Führer —the interview has already been prepared, and leaflet copies are ready for distribution throughout France. Documents which prove the insidious influence of Churchill will be reproduced. There is even a report of Churchill's instructions to de Gaulle, instructions to destroy Dakar at all costs. It is said that de Gaulle rejected them. You understand, my dear Baron?'

'I understand.' I felt a glow almost of comradeship for von Stroem. 'We are to undermine the growing belief in the strength of the Free French Forces.'

'It is but one duty,' said von Stroem. 'We shall say that de Gaulle has attempted to negotiate with the Führer but that Churchill had sabotaged those negotiations. All that Mondel is to publish, in papers which will be circulated the length and breadth of France. It will show how the Führer has been misrepresented, even by the Vichy Government. It will demand a new Government . . .'

'I imagine that Mondel will be its President,' I said.

'That is so.'

'And you are afraid that Murdoch will succeed in preventing this meeting between the Führer and Mondel?'

'And that he will endeavour to stop the publication of the interview,' said von Stroem.

I stared at him, my eyes reflecting the coldness in my mind.

'How is that possible?' I demanded. 'Murdoch might kill Mondel—such things happen. But the interview can be printed, whether it takes place or not.'

'It can, my dear Baron. But you do not fully understand the situation. You have been out of touch with events for so long. Mondel is a cunning man. When first the interview was suggested he agreed; then he disappeared.'

I sat back abruptly in my chair, and the movement gave me a twinge of pain which made my voice even louder.

'Can a man disappear without trace when he is of such importance? How has it happened? Where were the guards who watched him?'

'Mondel had prepared his disappearance for some time,' said von Stroem suavely. 'It was well-planned. He realised the possibility that his death before the publication of the interview would give added force to it, and he has made sure that no accident can happen.'

I stared at him coldly.

'I do not altogether understand you, von Stroem. You are first afraid that Murdoch will kill Mondel . . .'

'That is not so,' objected von Stroem. 'I am afraid that he will endeavour to prevent both the interview and the publication, and that he will contrive to get Mondel out of the country. The financial interests in Mondel's papers are in his own control, and his finances are secure in neutral countries. Mondel arranges for so much credit to be released each week—without this the papers could not be published. You see,' added von Stroem softly, 'Mondel has not been careless.'

I nodded slowly.

'It is so,' I said. 'Money, money—always that is the problem, it has been so since I can remember.' I pulled myself to my feet with a considerable effort, and regarded von Stroem evenly. 'I will examine the evidence.'

He bowed from the waist, collected his hat, stick and gloves from my desk, and turned to the door.

'I shall expect you at the Hôtel de Ville, Vichy,' he said. 'From there I am operating. And before then I shall have given a toast to your successful re-entry in the affairs of the Fatherland.' He clicked his heels again, turned, and went out; and two minutes afterwards I saw his car, the middle of three, disappearing beyond the open gates. I saw my guards close the gates after him, the sun glinting on their bayonets.

It did not seriously occur to me that von Stroem would make the statement without first verifying it. Somewhere

17

in France was Murdoch, and somewhere in France was my opportunity for revenge, a chance both to further Germany's cause and to avenge the injury which he had done to my reputation. I remember that my lips set in a smile, and it was then that I recalled that I had not been amused for a long time. I pressed one of the five bells set in my desk, and waited for Elsa to come.

She had retired with me.

I know of no woman but her whom I would trust; there are in fact occasions when I am troubled because of my reliance on her. But for my infirmity, which makes normal life impossible, she would have shared my bed. As it is I believe there is in her an affection for me which cannot be explained by normal loyalties, and because of that affection I trust her; she has never failed me. I was finding relish in the anticipation of telling her of our new opportunity, but slowly my smile disappeared. She had been overlong in coming; I do not like dilatoriness, and she should have been at hand, waiting for my summons.

I pressed the bell again, and then glanced down at the file on my desk. The crumpled photograph of Mary Dell had made the top cover of the file open.

She appeared to be mocking me, as if she knew why Elsa had not appeared.

For a period which seemed interminable I waited with my finger on the bell-push. In Elsa's room, not far from mine, I knew the bell was ringing stridently; all the bells in my home are strident, for thus quicker service is obtained.

I pushed the cover of the file down, and placed a book upon it. Still I could see the mocking eyes of the woman Dell, and I cursed her above my breath. But gradually I grew simply angry that Elsa should be so long in answering. I scoffed at my momentary fears.

It was a time of the day when Elsa should be in her room; there was no excuse for her not coming at once. I withdrew my finger, spent a moment in consideration, and then slowly I dragged myself to my feet, and took my stick from the hook. Laboriously I walked to the door, opened it, and stepped into the passage. I had decided to walk and not send Fritz with a message, for the pain of walking would strengthen my anger, so that I would not be tempted to overlook Elsa's dilatoriness.

I reached the door.

It had not opened, and I could not understand that, for the *thump—thump—thump* of my left foot and my stick made it impossible for me to approach quietly.

I stood on my left leg while I opened the door, and then I pushed it wider open with my stick.

It is a pleasant room; Elsa has a fondness for green, and I see no reason why her whims should not be indulged if they do not interfere with my preferences or my plans. The sun which had glinted on the bayonets of the guards was shining then through a partly open window, making the green of the curtains lighter than it really was. A gentle wind stirred the light fabric. In one corner there was her desk—and it pleases her to have that yellow. There was her typewriter, and in it a letter which I had dictated earlier in the day. There was her handkerchief, crumpled on the desk, as if she had dropped it there carelessly.

I cannot explain the tension which gripped me.

I can only say that I felt my heart beating fast and the constriction in my throat which comes so often when I am forced to make a movement. I felt that I could not breathe freely. I could not even find the strength to push the door open more widely and for some seconds I rested heavily on my stick, the breath coming noisily through my open mouth. I lurched forward so that my weight pushed the door open, then stood staring down at Elsa.

She was on the floor behind the door, her head and shoulders resting awkwardly against a couch.

Her eyes were closed; I could not be sure that she was breathing. I saw those things, and also the letter which she had crumpled in her right hand.

3

The Letter

I forgot that I had been angry.

I forgot everything but the fact that Elsa was lying unconscious, and that her colour, usually deep, had drained from her face. My eyes turned towards the letter, and then would not go away. I felt the weakness in my right side developing so that I knew that if I did not lean against a chair I should fall. I staggered to the nearest chair, but fell as I lowered myself into it. The pain was excruciating, but I did not cry out.

There were bells on her desk, as on mine, and by stretching out my stick I could touch one which would summon Fritz. I did so. Hardly had the ferrule of the stick come from the press than I heard a door open, and Fritz's footsteps padded along the carpeted passage. I heard him draw in a deep breath as he saw the open door, and before he came into sight I said:

'Bring me the serum from my desk.'

Fritz advanced a step into the room. I have seen him startled and surprised, frightened and cowering, but I have never seen him so dumbfounded. He stared at me as if he had not heard my order. I do not think he saw Elsa; his surprise at finding me in her room, which I never visit, made him oblivious to all else.

'You heard my order!' I shouted at him. 'Must I watch you gape, you doddering fool!'

'I—I regret, Excellency, I regret!' He turned and hurried away.

I had not used the serum for nearly a year. In that time I had not known what it was to be without pain for five consecutive minutes; even in my sleep I was conscious of it, although as with many afflictions long use can become an opiate.

The serum would stimulate my withered nerves and muscles for perhaps an hour. In that hour I must do the work that it would normally take a week. My mind refused to stay in contemplation of any one thing. Although the letter was within reach of my left hand, I did not move to take it.

Fritz returned.

I can inject in myself, but I prefer others to do it. I pulled up the sleeve of my right arm, and Fritz wiped a little patch clean with iodine. His old, rheumy hands were a little unsteady, and he pricked me twice with the needle.

'You clumsy fool!' I shouted. 'It is time I had a change of servant, that I can see.'

'I—I am sorry, Excellency,' he muttered, and he jammed the needle home. Except for the pain of the puncture, I felt little. He did not need to be told what to do next, but unbuttoned a side-flap in the waistband of my trousers. My clothes are made so that I need not disrobe for an injection to be given both to my arm and my thigh. He did a good job that time, and when he withdrew the needle, began to apologise again.

'I was afraid, Excellency. You are not well, I . . .'

'If I were not well that is all the more reason why you should be careful,' I told him. 'Bring coffee to me. Strong, black coffee. '

'At once, Excellency.'

The old fool was glad to get away, and when he had closed the door I smiled at it. It was good to see men trembling—I, physically so helpless, more infirm even than they realised, could make them afraid. It was good to feel the power over life and death.

I have always felt that.

A new strength was beginning to flow through me. I could *feel* it. I would be a fit man for that brief hour, within ten minutes of the injection.

I would not waste those ten minutes.

I allowed myself five by the watch on Elsa's desk, then turned again to her. My first act was to push my stick away. At such moments my hatred for the stick is a living thing. I let it fall to the floor before bending over Elsa. She was breathing, for her breast was rising and falling steadily. I straightened her a little, so that she was not so uncomfortable. I believed she had fainted, although I could understand nothing which could have induced such a condition.

At last I took the letter.

I did not know what was going to happen; had I been told it was possible, I would have laughed the suggestion to scorn. But I looked down at the small, neat handwriting, I read the words, and felt as weak as before the serum—as weak as when I had collapsed into the chair.

For I was reading in English!

I can read English—and for that matter a dozen languages—without difficulty. In the past year I had studied those languages and perfected my knowledge of them, although my accent is never good. I cannot control my vocal chords, although in my youth I could have passed muster for an Englishman anywhere in England. But I could still read it as well as my own language.

There was handwriting like this in Mary Dell's file; *she* had written this letter.

Slowly, I read the letter for the first time. As I read it I imagined I could hear the voice of the woman, as if she were speaking them to me; I could even detect the note of laughter.

It read:

Elsa, my dear,

I was grieved that you had been forced into retirement. I wonder whether you will come out of it with von Horssell? I think I hope you will.

How do you like the enclosed? It is effective isn't it? I wish it would last until we meet again, but I feel you will recover before that.

In case you could have forgotten me, I will sign myself with my maiden name—

Mary Dell!

I knew at once that its significance was not in the words —they were little more than an empty challenge, and neither Bruce Murdoch nor his wife would write such a letter for the sake of it. The real significance might be in the mentioned enclosure, or might be between the lines—or more subtle still, something there only for me to guess. I looked for the enclosure, and found a small fragment of rubber, of the kind which used to be used on carnival balloons at a time when such frivolities were considered necessary.

It was close to Elsa's shoulder.

I was so unused to moving without effort or pain that I staggered, but soon recovered and bent down and picked up the envelope.

The letter had been posted from Vienna the previous night. The franking was quite plain. The writing there was not Mary Dell's; and I knew it was not Murdoch's.

The first and most obvious possibility was that Mary Dell was in Vienna—or had been when she had written that letter. However, she could have posted it, or sent it by divers channels, to the actual sender in Vienna. That city is riddled with spies. I do not believe they constitute a menace to the rule of the Third Reich, but it needs a considerable force of men to repress their activities. Sir Robert Holt, the English director of S.1 Intelligence Branch in London had an organisation which I knew to be second only to my own at its best—and to that of the Gestapo in the countries which we occupy.

I stepped to the telephone, lifted it, and was immediately put through to the Chief of Police in Vienna. I gave instructions comprehensively. There was an English woman in the city, a spy who had arrived recently—within the past month. She must be found. The reputation of a Chief of Police who could permit the entry of such a woman was suspect. If he wished to avoid a formal inquiry he would search at once, and find the woman. I expected results before midnight.

'Yes, your Excellency,' he said. 'If she is here we will find her, Your Excellency, but I hope Your Excellency does not dispense with the possibility that she might not be within my jurisdiction. The Gestapo ...'

'Don't talk—find her!' I rasped.

I rang off, and as I did so Elsa's eyes began to open. They watered a great deal, but gradually opened wide. I was interested to know whether the fragment of rubber explained her collapse, or whether the letter could have induced a faint; I doubted the latter. I saw her eyes distend when she saw me standing in front of her without my stick, and the

23

effect was amusing. She scrambled at once to her feet, or she attempted to. There was weakness in her—the kind of weakness which I knew so well. For the moment our positions were reversed: I enjoyed that knowledge, and I laughed at her.

'Be careful, Elsa! You will soon need a stick if you fall like that.'

With the help of a chair she pulled herself to her feet. In falling, her frock was disarranged; it had buttons down its full length, and at the neck several buttons were unfastened. Her figure is well developed; I have heard it said that she is a Venus of form. I did not look at her eyes.

'Ludvic,' she said. 'You—you are standing!'

'Ach, am I surrounded with nothing but fools?' I demanded roughly. 'Yes, I am standing. Are you drunk that you should forget that I can stand for less than an hour? What happened to you?'

She licked her lips, which are very red.

'I—I do not remember. I had a letter . . .'

'Yes,' I said. 'You opened it. What then?'

Her nose and lips were puffy, like one who has been chloroformed, and for the first time I felt that I need not reprimand her.

'Yes, I opened it. I felt . . .' Her eyes narrowed, and she looked away from me towards the letter in my hand. 'I felt as if my breath was taken from me. I heard a faint noise first.'

'Yes, yes,' I said. 'There was a small balloon in the letter, and it burst when you opened it. There was gas, of course, it would have such an effect. You should have greater care in opening letters.' I handed the missile to her. 'Where is the von Stroem file?'

She was quickly recovering, for she moved to a steel filing cabinet near the door, opened it with a key which she took from her desk and put her hand on the file immediately.

I sat at her desk, and took the file.

I did not look at her, although I heard her breathing quicken as she read, and knew that she was feeling much as I had when first I had seen the letter.

I looked through the von Stroem dossier, and was grati-

24

fied to find that there was little I did not remember. He was from Saxe-Coburg-Gotha. He had served in the war of 1914–18 in the Air Arm. He had been educated at Heidelberg. He had been amongst the few Junkers-class supporters of the Nazi Party, and had been amongst the speakers at the Munich beer-cellar fiasco—that was a mistimed venture which I had condemned plainly; my own association with Party was not generally known until 1932.

In the Party, von Stroem had graduated from the Army to the Secret Branch because of his part in betraying Hess to the Leader. von Stroem had once been a close friend of Hess; his betrayal was an admirable thing, and it had served to prove the warmth of his devotion.

There followed many details of his activities, including the fact that he had torpedoed a troop-carrier—Elsa did not allow her records to become obsolete. There was a hundred such incidents showing his ruthlessness.

There was also a smaller dossier of his assistants; it was clear that he trusted few, and I had to agree that was wise. Four were mentioned. Two had been executed for suspect disloyalty. One had died two years before. The fourth, named Karl Lirchner, had been killed in a car accident three months before.

Three months—about the time that Murdoch had reached France.

I looked sharply at Elsa.

'Who replaced Lirchner in von Stroem's staff?'

She did not immediately reply, but before I repeated the question more abruptly she said:

'He had appointed no one up to a week ago, Excellency.' I was glad to note that she did not need to be told to suspend the use of my Christian name while we were so occupied; such familiarity was not wise. 'Excellency—this *must* mean that the woman has been able to contact with Vienna. She may even be in the country.'

As she spoke I realised something which I had missed before; I think the only reason I had not realised it was that the double shock of my rehabilitation and the news of Murdoch, added to the discovery of finding Elsa unconscious, had disorganised my mind.

Mary Dell had expected me to be at work again. The

letter, written at the latest the previous afternoon, was proof of that. She had known that I would be working *before von Stroem's visit*.

She must have known that von Stroem was coming to see me the day before his visit materialised; therefore she had access to his plans.

4

I Begin to Search

I looked across at Elsa, and I saw that she remained distraught. She was still suffering from the effect of the gas, and consequently I felt that it would be best if she rested a while.

'Go to your room, Elsa,' I said. 'Close your eyes for half an hour. Have Fritz call you at the end of that time, and come back here.'

Elsa did not immediately go. She is the one person on my entourage who does not immediately obey my orders, but she has a shrewd mind of her own, and I have often found that it has been advantageous to indulge her. It is perhaps a bad policy; but then, few men can be as dependent on a woman as I am.

Before I could repeat my instructions Fritz came in, after tapping on the door. He was much more composed, although his hand trembled as he began to pour out my coffee.

'I will do that,' said Elsa. 'Bring another cup, Fritz.'

'At once, Fräulein.' Fritz gave me the impression that he was glad to get out of the room. I watched Elsa pour out my coffee. It was some of a store which I had been wise enough to buy years before the outbreak of the war, for I remember the food shortages of the previous war only too well. She is fair, with long hair which does not curl on its own. She plaits it and coils it about her head. Her features are good, and she has the peculiar fair skin of the true Aryan. She has large grey eyes which have somewhat heavy lids. I think I have mentioned that her lips are very red, and her mouth large; a large mouth is a good sign in a woman; it tells of a capability for passion.

Her hand was steady as she handed me the coffee.

Fritz returned, and she poured herself a cup, drinking it slowly. Although I was sitting and drinking also, my mind was very active. Normally it is inclined to work slowly, although with a certainty that is essential to my work; after I have received my treatment I always feel that I can think four times as clearly and as fast.

'How can she have known you were likely to operate?' asked Elsa suddenly. And then: *'Are* we to work, Excellency?'

'Yes, and at once. The first thing of importance is for you to find out who posted that letter. I have telephoned the Vienna Chief of Police, but the fool will endeavour to protect himself rather than devote his full efforts to finding the woman. And, of course, we want Murdoch.'

'They are as much one as you and I,' remarked Elsa. She did not ask a series of foolish questions, but finished her coffee quickly and stood up. 'I will go to Vienna,' she said.

'You have two hours. At the end of those two hours you will be back in this room. We are flying to Vichy. On your way arrange for my machine to be brought to the landing-field so that we can go without attracting too much attention.'

'I will do that,' she promised.

She left her office, while I gave further attention to the servant Lirchner, who had died in a car accident while travelling with von Stroem. I found a note to that effect at the back of the dossier. It changed the idea which I had immediately had—that von Stroem and reason for doubting the faithfulness of Lirchner, and consequently had eliminated him. von Stroem's personal involvement in the accident made that unlikely.

The report said that the car had fallen over a small bridge across the Seine—a bridge which, like so many, had been weakened by saboteurs. There was nothing to suggest that the accident had been directly aimed at von Stroem.

27

Only three suspects had been arrested, and the suspicion against them was so slight that they had been sent to a concentration camp. I judged that von Stroem had not seriously considered the possibility that anyone had been involved; had there been suspicion he would have shot them out of hand.

They had been imprisoned as an example, of course.

The reports which constantly came from France had told me that the peasants particularly were more afraid of the concentration camp than of death. I do not think they show bad sense there—a dog would prefer a quick death to torture.

von Stroem, then, had sent three men away as examples to frighten others from similar acts of sabotage. And as far as Elsa had yet learned, he had no one to replace Lirchner.

von Stroem, as I have said, did not surround himself with a large bodyguard except on official occasions. So much of his work is secret that he needs to move alone, or almost alone. He needed someone like Lirchner, however, and I wondered if he knew of a man who could be trusted implicitly. If he did not, I had one on my staff who would act admirably, and at the same time report to me on any action von Stroem took without my knowledge. It is as well to know what is happening all the time.

I sent for Brunning.

He entered Elsa's room without knocking, which I considered bad. He should knock always. He is tall, fair, with a fine, straight-backed head and somewhat slanting forehead. His blue eyes are over-bold when he is looking at anyone but me His mouth is not well shaped but is strong and masculine; so is his chin, which had an ugly sabre wound on the left side. He is clean-shaven, with a long upper lip; and his nose is broad and short, with the nostrils slightly flattened.

Except for myself, I know of no man with more powerful hands. They are large, the fingers long as well as thick, and there is a matt of yellow hair at the back of them. He is something of a ladies' man; his square-topped fingers are always well-manicured, and there is usually a faint scent of perfume about him.

28

He was startled to see me in Elsa's chair.

'Excellency! A thousand apologies. I thought . . .'

'You thought you would find the Fräulein here,' I said. 'You will be wise to remember the need for announcing your arrival, Brunning, whether at my office or the Fräulein's. Attend, now. We are travelling to Vichy in one hour and fifty minutes. A 'plane will be here to take us. You will pack yourself, then arrange for me also to be packed.'

He took a step forward, his eyes glowing.

'We are at work, Excellency!'

'We are at work,' I agreed. 'Get those things done.'

'At once, Excellency!' He bowed from the waist, and went out. He had not given the Party salute, or said 'Heil Hitler'; that is a thing which I do not have in my own house, although beyond its confines all of my servants are most punctilious about observing the custom.

When Brunning had gone, I stood up without effort and stepped to the window. It was as perfect a day as one could wish. I think, however, that had it been raining in torrents, or snowing, or blowing a gale, I would have loved it that day. The false strength was in my veins, and a new day had dawned.

I was still disturbed by the knowledge which Mary Dell clearly had of von Stroem's plans, and it was a matter I could only take up with von Stroem himself. I decided, however, that I would do well to go into Vienna, and to make further inquiries myself. I rang for Fritz, and told him to have my car taken to the front immediately.

My room is on the ground floor, but as I was certain to be back within the hour, I did not take my stick but walked unaided. Servants appeared at all doors and passages, bowing and smiling their congratulations.

'May it last long, Excellency!'

'It gives us joy, Excellency!'

'The good God be praised, Excellency.'

Joachim, who is my chauffeur as well as the pilot in any air journey, is more familiar with the hours which I have free from paralysis, but even his heavy features lighted up.

'The Chief of Police,' I said to him.

He bowed, tucked a rug about my knees, and drove at good speed along the mountain road to Vienna. It takes little more than twenty minutes. All the time my mind was working at a speed which it had long since forgotten.

I saw Elsa's car, a cream-coloured Mercedes, outside the police building. As Joachim slowed down, Elsa came from the doorway. She immediately crossed to me.

'The letter was posted at a box on the outskirts of the city, Excellency. As always, the franking was done with a special stamp, so that if necessary letters could be traced. I am about to go there.'

'I will come,' I said.

I found the policeman a fool. He was frightened at the sight of me, and he stammered as he spoke. Of course he maintained that he knew everyone who posted letters in that box. He did not think that many had been posted yesterday.

'Think!' I barked. 'You say you are sure you see them all, and you "think" there were few! You will have to learn to be more sure, dolt. Call on your memory! Who posted letters?'

'I can recall the Gauleiter, Excellency...'

'You dull-witted swine!' I said. 'Am I asking questions for the sake of it? Which women used the box?'

'There were a number, Excellency.'

'Were there strangers amongst them?' asked Elsa.

'I—I noticed none, Fraulein.'

'It would not be posted by a stranger,' I said. 'Have the sense to realise that, Elsa. They would not draw attention to themselves in such a way. But there is no time for further inquiry here.' I raised a clenched fist in front of the fool's face. 'In one hour you will have written the names of all who used this post box last evening. You understand?'

'I will endeavour...'

'You will do it!' I roared at him, and the fool shrunk back, afraid of what would happen if he failed. I was sure that he would remember before the night was out. I told him to take the list in person to the police building, and told him also to mention my name.

In the car, I said to Elsa: 'We can arrange for the interrogations to be carried out in Vienna. Any who are suspect can be sent then to Vichy.'

30

'That is so,' she agreed.

She had left her car in the road outside the police building, and consequently she sat next to me. At the end of the street where the policeman was watching my car were several other vehicles, and some fool failed to see the badge on my radiator which gives me right of way. Consequently Joachim was forced to stop. It was a cold afternoon, and the sun which had earlier been at its best had gone behind a cloud. As I sat fuming at the delay, an old woman approached the car and dared to open the door.

A filthy old crone.

There was a vile smell from the cotton shawl draped about her shoulders, and her nose was running. Her face was red with the cold, but I knew that she could have worn warmer clothes had she so desired: mendicants will always take advantage of difficult times.

'Good evening, Excellency,' she said in a high, sing-song voice, and in a scraggy hand with long, black-filled nails, she extended a box of matches. 'Buy a match from a poor old soul, Excellency. The wind cuts through me, each pfennig I earn ...'

'Go away at once!' Elsa ordered.

'Just one pfennig, Excellency ...'

Joachim was then able to restart the car, and he did so: had he not known that I was in a considerable hurry he would have dealt with the beggar himself. As it was, I leaned forward and slammed the door on the wretch. She started back, screaming; the door had caught her finger.

'It will teach her wisdom,' I growled.

'She needs it,' Elsa said.

As Joachim turned the car into the main thoroughfare there was a shouting from the pavements, and people waved and gesticulated, all in the direction of the car. Joachim rightly ignored them and increased his speed, but into the car there came shrieks and cries, high-pitched and displeasing.

Elsa looked out of her window, and then spoke into the mouthpiece to Joachim.

'Stop immediately,' she said, without consulting me.

Joachim did as she told him, and then Elsa opened the door I had recently closed. For the first time I saw that the

31

cotton shawl of the old woman had caught in the handle, and she had been dragged with the car! Her face was torn and bleeding, and one of her hands was also cut, but I felt a searing anger at the delay which she had caused.

But I heard also an angry murmur from the crowd.

I do not excuse it: I know that during the previous winter there had been much hardship, more perhaps in Vienna and in other Austrian towns than in Berlin. It was inevitable, because of the accursed British blockade. There had been food riots, and an atmosphere of revolt which—I had thought—had been crushed. But on occasions it would flare up again, the sullen, usually unspoken, hostility of the swine of the streets—the social-democrats and communists who would not dare to reveal themselves in normal times, but did occasionally grow forgetful and risk being thrown into concentration camps.

Had I not been in a hurry I would have dealt with them myself.

As it was, I raised my voice to attract the attention of four S.S. men who were on the other side of the road. Rightly, they had shown no interest in the old woman, their duty being confined to keeping order. But at my summons they came running, drawing their rubber truncheons.

'The wretched Jew accosted me,' I told them, pointing at the old woman, over whom three or four people were bending. 'Take her away—have her punished.'

'A Jew!' cried one of the S.S. men. 'A stinking Jew!'

They moved the crowd, and I spared a moment to admire the vigour with which they did so. Men and women hurried off in all directions and the old crone was left lying in the roadway. Her eyes were open; she was not so badly hurt as she wanted to make out. The S.S. men hauled her to her feet, and she began to cry aloud, cursing me and all those with me. One man silenced her with a blow across the mouth, but she continued to glare at me, and she spat —a blob of saliva mixed with blood hit the glass of the door as Elsa closed it. Joachim drove on immediately, and I said:

'I shall need to talk to the Chief of Police on my return, Elsa. They are slack here.'

'It is so,' said Elsa.

32

It was necessary to go to the police building for her car, although I did not propose to interview the officials then. We drew up behind her car, and Elsa climbed out, saying:

'I will follow you immediately, Excellency. Please do not delay.'

'That was not my intention,' I said.

While I spoke to her, Joachim had cleaned the window: I was glad that the stain had gone. There was no sense in my thinking twice about the incident, but for a moment it had been disturbing.

Suddenly, Joachim stopped at a sign from Elsa. I saw him looking towards her, and following his gaze I saw Elsa standing motionless by the open door of her car, in her right hand a slip of paper.

It was as if she was still holding the letter which Mary Dell had sent her, and I was more perturbed than I was ready to admit. I tapped sharply on the window, so that Joachim hurried to open the door. Elsa stepped to me. For the second time that day she had lost her colour, and she handed me the paper without saying a word.

For the second time that day I saw Mary Dell's writing. There was just one sentence:

How do you like being hated, Elsa

5

The Chief of Police

That was the first time I realised how gravely certain things had deteriorated in Greater Germany. I believe that there is good reason for my lack of knowledge. Prior to my retirement, I had operated outside of the Fatherland and had accepted the word of Himmler and Goebbels that the home situation was well in hand. True, there were spies, and there were saboteurs, but I had not considered it possible for anyone to place such a note on the seat of a car standing outside the police building.

Yet Elsa had found it there.

Worse, it was clear that the note had recently been written. The ink was a faint blue, newly blotted. Mary Dell had written it within the past two or three hours.

It was no longer possible for me to postpone my interview with the Chief of Police. I walked immediately to the main doors, and along the passages to his office, which was on the first floor. Elsa and Joachim were making inquiries in the car park.

Outside Erich von Gletten's door was a tall, pale-faced man whose round shoulders and thin chest did not please me; he had clearly failed to take advantage of the opportunities for physical culture which the Party provided.

He did not move aside as I approached the door.

'I wish to enter,' I stated.

The man still did not move. He swallowed, and moved his Adam's apple as he did so. His voice was high-pitched and I disliked that also.

'I regret, Excellency, Baron von Gletten is engaged.'

'Move aside,' I growled. 'Are you blind that you do not recognise me?'

Again his Adam's apple moved as he swallowed.

'Of course, Excellency, His Excellency the Baron von Horssell, who could fail to recognise you? But the Baron ˙ . .'

I moved the man aside with my left hand, and he winced at the grip of my fingers. I ignored his protests. If this was the service and respect I could expect to obtain from von Gletten, a change in the police at Vienna was essential.

The door opened freely.

I stepped through, first seeing von Gletten, who is a grossly fat man. He is also short, and that exaggerates the size of his waistband, which is truly colossal. I have a prejudice against small men in any case, and with von Gletten there was the additional factor of a completely bald head. It is small and egg-shaped, except at the back which steeps deeply to his neck—or more correctly his shoulders, for he gives one the impression of having no neck. He has, however, a prodigiously big and fleshy chin. Beneath his small brown eyes are purplish bags, signs of heavy and fast living. I know that von Gletten is a homosexual, but I will

34

not speak of some of the inhabitants of his large and luxurious house on the outskirts of the city.

This gross fellow started to his feet.

'Excellency! I gave orders ...'

Then I saw von Stroem.

It gave me a turn, although there was perhaps no reason why it should. von Stroem had not, after all, said that he was to return immediately to Vichy, but merely that he had many things to do and must leave me quickly. I do not know whether he was surprised to see me: if he was he did not show it.

'It is all right, von Gletten,' he said, and the Chief of Police subsided in his chair. There was a fringe of sweat on his purply under-lip, and his eyes looked frightened. I do not wonder; if von Stroem was questioning him, he had reason to be. 'I am delighted to see you again, my dear Baron,' von Stroem went on suavely. 'And you are so well!'

I hated him for that remark.

'It will not last,' I said. 'But I can arrange for periods of physical fitness—perhaps you did not know.'

'I had heard of it, my dear Baron, but I was not aware that it could be so effective.'

'I came to see von Gletten,' I said. 'I talked to him on the telephone a short while ago—have you had results?' I stared at the fat man, who took a brightly coloured silk handkerchief from his pocket, and dabbed at his forehead.

'Not—not yet, Excellency.'

'While the city is in the condition that I find it,' I said coldly, 'you are not likely to obtain results. It is possible that His Excellency Baron von Stroem was discussing such faults with you.'

'That is so,' said von Stroem. 'I was in the office when your call came, Baron. Dare I hope you have information about the woman Dell,'

'It is so,' I said. 'She is in Vienna.'

von Stroem swung about to face von Gletten, who was perspiring so quickly that he could not wipe his forehead and lips and keep them dry. I have rarely seen a man more frightened.

'But—but it is impossible!'

'The Baron does not lie!' barked von Stroem. 'The

35

woman is here—how has that been possible? Are not all immigrants kept segregated from the rest of the population until they have been vouched for? Is Vienna a hot-bed of vice and intrigue, of treachery and disloyalty? Is it conducted by a fool—or,' added von Stroem in a voice which he suddenly pitched on a lower key, 'by a rogue?'

'I—I am desolate,' gasped von Gletten. 'Everything is superintended by myself or my most trusted lieutenants. Only a woman of remarkable audacity could be in Vienna without sufficient authority. I swear by the Führer that I have neglected nothing!'

'The city is riddled with spies,' growled von Stroem, 'and with vice. I am told that there are brothels on the main streets—was that the case before you took charge?'

'It—it cannot be so,' gasped von Gletten. 'I would know of it. The moral standard of the city has never been higher . . .'

von Stroem sneered.

'I was accosted in my car a dozen times. It is a fine story. There will be an inquiry.'

'Excellency! I will have every man questioned . . .'

'There will be an inquiry,' I agreed. Particularly about the gross inefficiency of the guard outside your own building—yes, here!' I told them what had been found on the seat of Elsa's car.

'So she is here, and free,' von Stroem said softly.

'It would appear that she arrived because you were coming.'

'Perhaps she followed me,' said von Stroem.

'My information is that she was here before you,' I declared. I did not enlarge on that; the more he saw of the results which I could get the more impressed he would be. 'Every stranger who has entered the city in the past week must be questioned again. All who cannot give satisfactory answers must be detained.' I knew that von Gletten would take the instructions as a command in the desperate hope of saving himself from an inquiry.

'It will be started at once,' he promised.

'I shall expect quick results,' I said.

'I shall send for them tomorrow,' said von Stroem. He had put his hat, stick and gloves on von Gletten's desk.

He collected them, held them in an arm crooked against his chest, and extended his free arm. 'Heil Hitler!'

von Gletten sprang to his feet.

'Heil Hitler! And nothing shall be omitted, gentlemen.'

Neither von Stroem nor I troubled to reply.

The man with the Adam's apple neck was cringing outside when we left. We ignored him, and until we reached the front hall we did not speak. Then von Stroem said:

'Baron, what gave you the impression that Dell knew where I was coming?'

'I found a letter suggesting as much,' I said.

'That is most disturbing.'

'I knew that you would feel so.'

'It is particularly disturbing,' went on von Stroem softly, 'because only *I* knew where I was coming. That I would visit the Führer, yes, that was known. That I should call for your help—it was a thing only in my mind until I had permission from the Führer.'

'Do you know what you suggest?' I demanded stiffly.

'I am fully aware. That the news of my impending visit leaked out in Berchetsgarten. Do not imagine such a thing is impossible, Baron. The impending meeting between the Führer and Mondel was known only to the closely watched officials at Berchtesgarten, to myself—and to Mondel.'

'We shall find the truth,' I said. 'It will be of interest to discover if we are followed. I have arranged to leave for Vichy in one hour and fifteen minutes.'

'Then we shall be there almost together. You will make all arrangements to make sure that no one is able to follow you—or if they do so follow, to know who it is.'

'It is an elementary suggestion,' I said coldly.

'A thousand apologies, Baron!' The fellow even smiled. 'Before we part, there is one thing. I am not at all impressed by von Gletten.'

'I would have opposed his appointment here.'

'It will be wise if the appointment is changed immediately.'

'The sooner the better,' I agreed. 'If there is disloyalty in the man, there will be an opportunity for him to warn those for whom we are searching.'

'I shall recommend an immediate suspension,' said von

37

Stroem. 'For your sake alone, Baron, that was one of the objects of my visit here. I am recommending Wesser to replace him. You know of Wesser?'

I did; and I was surprised.

Wesser is a Bavarian who, at one time, wavered in his adherence to the Party and was once compelled to flee from Berlin, for his activities had been suspect with Himmler. Since then, however, he had returned to favour. That might heve been because he had influence with Goering, who I believe is a distant relative. But the latter's reputation, as I knew it, was what the English would call 'humanitarian.

'Is he the right man?' I asked.

'He has done good work,' said von Stroem, and again he smiled at me, as if suggesting that there were many things which I did not know. 'Until recently he was in Prague.'

'It is not for me to disagree,' I said.

'You must not be misled by the reports that he is well disposed towards certain non-Nazi principles,' said von Stroem. 'He has built up such a reputation carefully, finding that it enables him to get excellent results. I shall go to Berchtesgarten now, and from there proceed to Vichy.'

He bowed, and allowed me to walk ahead to my car.

By then I was feeling tired.

I was not pleased with the results of the past hour. I felt that much time had been wasted, and my energies while the effect of the serum lasted was invaluable. But the time had gone, and there was nothing I could do except admit that many things which were disturbing had happened.

I remembered suddenly that there was a question I had for him, and turned, to find von Stroem just behind me.

'von Stroem,' I said. 'There is one thing. You were unfortunate to lose your man, Lirchner.'

'That is so.'

'Is there another to replace him?'

von Stroem's lips curled in his detestable smile.

'And this is someone through whom the information could leak? No, my dear Baron, I can assure you that is not the case. I have dispensed with the services of those men who normally would be with me, my movements are too uncertain, and too private. I could trust Lirchner implicitly.'

I nodded: it was painful, and for the first time since the injection I felt a quickening beat at my heart. Before I reached my study I would need my stick. It would not be wise for me to stand much longer.

Nor was it the moment for recommending Brunning.

'Of your reputation I am well aware,' I said, and I climbed laboriously into the car. von Stroem clicked his heels, and went to his own car, a black Cadillac which he drove himself.

Elsa came forward.

'We have found nothing,' she said. She is never one to waste words.

'I did not expect it. Elsa . . .' I spoke hurriedly, seized with an idea which might yield results. 'Follow von Stroem. If he discovers you are following him, pretend to have a message from me. You will watch any who are in close attendance on him. You understand? And . . .' I hesitated, and closed my eyes, overcome by a wave of nausea, but it went. 'And there is another thing. We shall make von Stroem feel that he is in danger, personal danger. He will need a bodyguard. Brunning, I think, will serve.'

Elsa rested her hand on the back of mine. For the first time since I had found her unconscious I felt that she was fully capable of working at high pressure.

'Excellent,' she said. 'And I will find out another thing. Perhaps von Stroem is susceptible to women.'

I laughed; my weakness was not yet too great to prevent that.

'It has been known!' I conceded. 'Yes, it has been known more than once. Harken to me. Stay close to von Stroem until he leaves for Vichy. If you should be too late to come in my aeroplane, follow immediately. I shall stay at *l'Hôtel Grande*.'

'I will see you there,' she said.

I do not remember seeing her open the door of her car; she appeared to be in it and driving in the wake of von Stroem before Joachim let out the clutch of my car. I wished that hers was not cream, for it would be easily noticed; and then I smiled to myself, for I knew that I could rely on Elsa to be discreet in all things.

The journey to the house was not pleasant.

Apart from Mary Dell, there was the anxiety of von Gletten's loose control of Vienna: a change was certainly necessary, but was Wesser the man? At the moment at all events I could do nothing to alter that choice.

I was uncomfortable and tired as we climbed the hill leading to the house. I would need half an hour's complete rest before starting the journey. I closed my eyes in the car, then opened them at an exclamation from Joachim which reached me clearly.

I was in time to see a vivid red flash somewhere in the grounds followed by an explosion and a blast which made the car quiver.

I did not need to be told that the aeroplane, probably being refuelled after being taken from its hangar, had been destroyed in the grounds of my house.

6

I am Delayed

It is not possible for me to summarise my feelings when I saw the flames, and realised what had happened. But it is true to say that immediately I thought of Murdoch. That, adding to the fast-fading efforts of the serum, combined to make me physically very cold. I sat huddled in the corner of the car, staring towards the fire while Joachim slowed down, and then opened the glass partition for instructions. Normally I do not like the partition opened. It is of bullet-proof glass, and affords a measure of protection which I feel is necessary.

'Drive to the scene,' I ordered.

Joachim slid the partition to immediately and, a few yards along the drive, turned left onto the strip, which had been constructed in the hillside at considerable expense. Austrian labourers did most of the work, soon after the

Anschluss. The fire was increasing, and I could see several men working near it in an endeavour to put out the flames, but it was a hopeless task.

It was then that I was suddenly conscious of danger. I have felt the same before, and have never known myself wrong. There was danger close at hand, urgent and personal. I saw two men approaching the car, which was slowing down as it drew near the flames. They had no business to leave their work of fire-fighting. Immediately I pressed the bell which connects with the driving-seat—giving two short rings which tells Joachim of approaching danger.

He did not need further telling.

He turned the wheel of the car, and increased speed at the same time. I saw one of the two men level something towards me, and saw also the stab of yellow flame which followed. I heard the *ping!* of a bullet against the glass.

I crouched low.

My right side was seized with cramp and the wasted muscles twitched. I had to clench my teeth with the effort to withstand the pain. There was nothing I could do to defend myself if Joachim was hurt, although I knew that he would give his life for me. It was one of those moments when I would have given all my worldly fortune for the strength and freedom of a normal man.

But the danger did not last long.

That was as much because the two men wished to make good their escape as to the speed with which Joachim took his revolver from the holster fitted into the side of the driving-door. I saw both men running towards the high wall which runs about the estate, and I straightened up, watching them and watching also the several guards who were rushing towards them, firing as they ran.

I cursed those guards.

Not only had they allowed strangers within the gates, but they had permitted shooting to take place, had allowed my life to be endangered. I recognised them. Hans Leiber, Otto Glebb, and a man named Ritzler. Big, heavy men, with years of service in the Party; this was an error they would regret.

But I acknowledged their tactical cleverness.

They did not run in the same direction; one followed the

41

two racing men towards the wall, another made for the main gate to cut off any attempt to run that way, and the third towards a smaller gate some hundred yards away. But despite the fact that they maintained their firing the two fugitives were not hurt; those men, in fact, zig-zagged to avoid the shots as if unaware of the high wall which confronted them.

I wondered who they were.

I knew that Murdoch worked with two Englishmen named Angell and Fuller, Angell a thin man and tall, Fuller much shorter and stocky; the fugitives measured approximately to those descriptions. Except for Murdoch and Dell, there were no people in the world I would rather have in my control.

I pulled the mouthpiece of the speaking-tube to me.

'Drive towards them,' I told Joachim, and he eased off the brakes as if he had anticipated my instructions.

I now felt sure that there was no way in which the fugitives could escape. I reached a spot within ten yards of the wall, and watched as they neared the wall fifty yards away. I grew more certain that they were Angell and Fuller, although both were dressed as Austrian peasants; and then I recalled that a number of peasants had recently been brought to the grounds to prepare the soil for the Autumn crop of fruit and vegetables.

'We will take the prisoners to my study,' I said to Joachim. 'There they will be questioned.'

'*Ja*, Excellency,' Joachim answered immediately. He was watching the chase as closely as I, and perhaps with the same feeling of satisfaction now that the danger was past.

It was then that I saw what I had considered the impossible.

Lieber, Glebb and Ritzler were now closing on the fugitives, who turned with their backs to the grey stone wall. That did not surprise me; the English will fight no matter what the odds. But these two put their hands to their pockets, and threw something at my guards. I saw only the small round objects curling through the air, and I thought at first of hand-grenades or small bombs, but the explosions that might have been expected did not materialise. Instead there were clouds of whiteish vapour which app-

42

eared suddenly about the heads of my guards as the missiles struck them.

I saw each guard collapse, much as Elsa must have collapsed when she had opened Dell's letter.

Meanwhile Angell and Fuller—I have since confirmed my suspicion of their identities—acted with a coolness which I was constrained to admire. Angell, using his height to advantage, threw a rope ladder to the top of the wall. Although the top was supposed to be quite smooth, to prevent such a contingency, a hook or nail had been placed in position, and the rope caught. Fuller scrambled up with the agility of a monkey, reached the top and dropped down the other side. Angell began to climb after him.

Then I saw Brunning.

I do not know what had brought him from the house, but he came at speed, carrying a sub-machine gun under his arm. He began to spray the wall about Angell's climbing figure, and I felt an urgent hope that the man would fall back.

He stopped moving for a moment, and lost his grip with his left hand. He was caught!

No—it was not to be so quick.

I cursed aloud as I saw him move again, still using only his right hand. Then Fuller appeared again at the top, perhaps summoned by a call for assistance. I do not know how Brunning had missed the targets as they both stood for a moment on the top of the wall; I do know that the Englishmen disappeared.

They did not take the ladder with them.

Brunning had not stopped moving, and he let the sub-machine gun fall as he reached the ladder, and began to climb up. By then other guards and mechanics from the aeroplane were rushing to his assistance.

Brunning reached the top of the wall, and began to shoot with a revolver taken from his holster. I could not hope to see whether he was successful. The lazy Austrians began to climb up the rope in his wake, but before they reached his side I heard clearly the start of a car engine on the far side of the wall.

I lifted the speaking-tube.

'My study,' I ordered.

I was too angry and infuriated to think clearly. Murdoch and his friends are virtually the only people I know who can make me feel like that. I sat back in the car, with my aching side a torment and my mind confused. Angell and Fuller had come to my grounds, had destroyed my aeroplane, shot at me, and then had escaped. The knowledge goaded me to a state nearly of frenzy, but on the short drive to the front of the house I controlled myself.

When I reached the house Joachim hurried from his seat.

'I will fetch your stick, Excellency.'

'It is in the Fraulein's study,' I said.

'Thank you, Excellency.'

He hurried inside, and returned very quickly with my stick. Then he helped me out. It was useless for me to try to walk, and Joachim had anticipated that, also, for from the house came Fritz, pushing the wheel chair in which I am so often forced to travel.

I lowered myself into it, and was pushed into the house —the approach to which is on a gentle slope, and with no steps, because of my preference of wheeling myself in and out. I was pushed to my room, and helped to the chair at my desk. My forehead was wet with sweat, and I felt choked.

'Coffee,' I croaked to Fritz.

He bowed and hurried off, while I regarded Joachim dully.

'I wish to see Brunning,' I said. 'Glebb, Ritzler and Lieber will be placed under close arrest until I have interrogated them. Hurry!'

'At once, Excellency!'

When the door had closed behind him, I looked out of my window. Dusk was beginning to gather, and that made the red glow from the fire more lurid. It flickered against the windows, and the dark walls of the study, an afterglow of the aeroplane in which, by then, I should have been on the way to Vichy. It would take at least an hour, perhaps two or three, for a replacement 'plane to be brought here. I had been delayed solely by the efforts of Angell and Fuller. Murdoch and Dell had contrived to prepare both an organisation and a plan of campaign which would give me a lot of trouble.

I heard footsteps outside the door, and called 'come in' before Brunning knocked. When he entered I was momentarily perturbed, for his face was dirty and bleeding a little.

'What happened to you?' I demanded.

'It is nothing, Excellency. I fell from the wall.'

'You must learn to be more sure-footed,' I said. 'We are facing a task which will not be made easier by mistakes.'

'I will, Excellency.' Brunning paused, and I waited for him to go on. There is no room for sentiment in matters of this nature; he had failed to prevent the escape of the fugitives, and it was his duty to report and to explain. He continued: 'When I reached the top of the wall, the shorter man was helping the other into the car. There was a woman at the wheel. She was hatless, and her hair was long.'

'Dark hair,' I said.

'No, Excellency. She was fair—as fair as the Fräulein.'

I brooded for some moments, while Brunning stood stiffly at attention in front of me. I looked at him, but did not see him. It was folly to imagine that because the colour of the hair was different that the woman had not been Dell. She would bleach it, of course, and thus help to disguise her appearance.

'Proceed,' I said.

'I fired four shots, Excellency, three times hitting the nearest wing of the car, but the tyres were hardly visible, they had special protection. My fourth bullet struck but did not break the window when I tried to shoot the woman. Before I could fire again, the man behind me lost his balance and tried to save himself by holding onto me.'

'Who was it?' I snapped.

'A mechanic—Schmidt by name.'

'Is he under guard?'

'No, Excellency, I thought—an accident . . .'

'Accident you fool!' I roared. 'He could have done that deliberately. Make sure! And make sure of these things also. Arrange for another aeroplane to replace that which is lost. Make full enquiries about the two men who escaped. Telephone the Chief of Police in Vienna to radio a report to Elsa and His Excellency the Baron von Stroem that I have been temporarily delayed. You understand all that?'

He clicked his heels.

'Fully, Excellency.'

'Proceed,' I said.

He had not been gone a moment before Fritz brought coffee, and it did a little to ease the pain in my side which, however, had passed its peak. I sat thinking of the most urgent problem—that of Mondel, in France. Until I could be reasonably assured that no direct efforts would be made on my life and Elsa's, the degree of danger was acute, and it lessened the prospects of a satisfactory way of finding the newspaper owner.

His meeting with the Führer was only three days distant.

Brunning returned in twenty minutes by the clock.

'I have carried out the instructions, Excellency. The aeroplane will be here at eight o'clock.'

'That is in more than an hour. Cannot it be quickened?'

'There was difficulty, Excellency.'

'With what?' I barked.

'Fuel for the machine,' said Brunning. 'It is not possible to keep many machines fuelled and ready for immediate service, or so I was informed by the airport.'

Petrol—it was always the same. Petrol was short, money was short. A thousand, ten thousand, aeroplanes were standing idle during the nights and a paltry few hundred were sent to raid Britain because of the shortage of fuel.

'Proceed,' I said.

'The two saboteurs were Austrian labourers, brought here for service a week ago, when twenty men were so employed. They were guarded by two S.S. members . . .'

'Which two members?'

'Lieber and Glebb, Excellency.'

'I shall deal with Lieber and Glebb,' I said.

'I have questioned Lieber. He tells me that the two men were the least troublesome in the fields, attending to their work without trying to find excuses for needless delays. Consequently he paid more attention to the more recalcitrant ones.'

'Consequently he relaxed his watch on the two, whereas he should have been more careful with them than the others,' I corrected. 'The slaves who work willingly are rogues or fools. I will see Lieber.'

'He is waiting outside, Excellency. The Austrian mechanic, Schmidt, is also outside. I have questioned him. He insists it was an accident.'

Lieber, too big a man to have brains, but until then believed a conscientious member of the Party, was pale and apprehensive. Schmidt, a much smaller man, was not pale; his cheeks were red with warm blood, and I knew that Brunning had not questioned him gently. There was a cut under his right eye, where the flesh hung on his cheek. His hands, too, were bloody.

He crept forward, cringing.

'Excellency . . .'

'Since when have you been told to speak first?' I roared at him, and Brunning pushed him towards my desk roughly. He staggered against it, and his blood-stained fingers gripped the side of the desk, soiling it with his foul blood. I picked a heavy paper-weight from the desk with my strong left hand and brought it down heavily on his fingers. He gasped, and snatched his hand away.

'Learn not to contaminate this room,' I said harshly. 'Why did you push Captain Brunning from the wall?'

'Excellency, I swear it was not so, I stumbled as any man might stumble! I beg you to believe me, Excellency!'

The man was telling the truth; I did not try to blind myself to that. But I did not say what I thought, and I turned to Lieber.

'And you?' I said. 'What lie will you tell? Why were you so long in following these spies?'

7

The Journey Begins

For some seconds Lieber did not speak, and I waited, watching him closely. My fear was that he was a traitor, that the other guards had deliberately worked with him to allow the two 'peasants' to escape, and that the shooting at me had been done with their connivance. But I did not think that as I listened to Lieber; there was no defiance in him.

'Excellency, I abase myself for my negligence, but it was not wholly my fault, that I swear. I needed two men to assist with the fuelling of the machine, and sent for men from the fields. These two were known to be industrious. Not until they began to hurry from the aeroplane did I suspect trouble. Then there was the explosion. Excellency, the blast threw me from my feet, and I was not able to give chase immediately. The same is true of Glebb and Ritzler . . .'

'I am questioning you.'

'Of course, Excellency, but—but they were under my orders, they came to the aeroplane at my instructions.'

'You are too thoughtful for your subordinates,' I told him.

'Yes, Excellency.'

'Go on,' I ordered him.

'Immediately after the explosion we hurried after the two men, Excellency. I had seen one stand back from the machine, and throw what appeared to be a small grenade into the cabin, as the petrol was being loaded. The petrol tank exploded immediately after the fire began.'

'Which man threw the grenade?'

'The taller, Excellency.'

It would be Angell. He had always been the man, after Murdoch, to act; Fuller was a support man. That is because Angell has the surer eye and is the quicker thinker.

'And what followed?' I asked.

'I saw them shoot at you, Excellency. Immediately I instructed Glebb and Ritzler to run in different directions to cut off the fugitives' escape. I ran directly at them—but they had the fortune of the devil.'

'They had the luck of the English,' I snarled at him. 'You may go. You will be more careful in future, and your fine friends. When I return I shall consider what disciplinary steps will be necessary.'

'I shall be careful, Excellency, my one concern is for

48

your safety.' He clicked his heels, saluted and turned away, very glad indeed to have escaped so lightly.

I turned my gaze to Schmidt.

'You will work in the fields,' I ordered. 'I need mechanics and guards who can be relied on not to make mistakes. Take him out, Herr Kapitän.'

'At once, Excellency.'

Brunning took Schmidt's arm and led him from the office; the Austrian also would realise that he might have suffered more than he had. But I believed him. He had stumbled, any man would clutch at another to save himself.

The fortune of the devil, Lieber had said.

The luck of the English, I had corrected him; but that was only half true. Angell and Fuller, Murdoch and Dell, did not rely so much on good luck; they planned too carefully, knew just what chances to take, and if there appeared the remotest hope of success, they would make their effort.

Where were they now?

It would be possible to have a countrywide search made for them, but I do not believe in wasting effort; they would have a place of security somewhere in the mountains. No, to search for them would be to waste time and thought.

For they would follow me.

That was the way to find them: lure them into my presence, to appear careless and to make it seem easy for them to approach me.

The shooting had not been wild and accidental when they had fired at me; they had deliberately tried to kill me. And they would again. I did not fear that they would succeed, but I knew that pretending carelessness, as a bait, it would be necessary for me to take extra precautions.

Elsa now would not travel with me.

Was it sufficient to take Brunning and Joachim?

As I hoped von Stroem would accept the offer of Brunning's services when he had received the fright which I proposed to prepare for him, Brunning might leave me in Vichy. I needed one other man.

In different circumstances I might have taken Lieber.

Most of the men who had worked for me in the past and who had experience of working in personal collaboration with me had been released when I had returned from

England; they could be of more service with the Gestapo and the Intelligence Service than with me. But I decided to send for one Karl Voss, to meet me in France.

Voss is young but I know of few cleverer men, although he gives many people the impression that he is a fool; I had the same impression when I first met him.

I telephoned immediately to Berlin; there were delays on ordinary calls, but mine were always answered promptly. The damage which the British have inflicted on the capital is exaggerated considerably in the American and other neutral Press—I need not waste time in denying the absurd claims which the British Bomber Command makes —but it is inevitable that sometimes there should be delay. I was fortunate, however, and was able to arrange for Voss to leave the following morning by air for Vichy.

Brunning came in shortly afterwards.

I had not yet given him an outline of what were the likely factors in the task which we faced, and I did so then. He had not met Murdoch or Dell or any of the others, and it is not my habit to talk of them, particularly to subordinates, although I would occasionally discuss them with Elsa. I began to outline something of Murdoch's methods, and was surprised when Brunning begged leave to interrupt.

'What is it?' I demanded.

'I should say, Excellency, that I have some knowledge of Murdoch and Dell.'

'How have you obtained it?'

'Through the Fräulein,' stated Brunning.

In such moments I have a way of making my face quite expressionless; I know that it disturbs those at whom I look. Also, by moving my lower jaw a little at the back, I cause my jaw-bones to move slightly, as if I am chewing.

I was not pleased. Elsa should not have discussed this with him or with anyone. I recalled that he had entered her office without knocking.

'Your association with the Fräulein appears to be somewhat intimate,' I said.

'I assure you, Excellency, it is one which considers only the best way of which we can be of service to you,' replied Brunning, but I thought the answer too swift and too

50

suave; I wondered, for the first time, whether there could be an *affaire* between Elsa and Brunning. The possibility displeased me; sentiment leads to weakness, almost without exception. Moreover, Elsa was mine, by duty, by affection. It was of no account that I was forced to live the life of a eunuch, although without the eunuch's utter lack of sexual excitement.

Elsa and Brunning? I cursed the man because I feared then that he had made advances towards her, that behind my back he had contrived to turn a business association into a love affair. Will men never learn that *all* of their lives must be devoted to the Fatherland, that they have no time for independent thoughts and emotions, love or hate?

I made no immediate comment, and Brunning continued:

'The Fräulein has always been perturbed, Excellency, by the misfortunes which overlook you in England. She has sought a way by which you could be avenged. We have both lived in the hope that you would be able to resume your contact with Murdoch and Dell. The more I knew of them the more service I could be in that eventuality—in *this* eventuality, Excellency.'

His face looked animated and eager.

I wondered if I had jumped to conclusions too freely. It was natural that Elsa should wish for a second opportunity to work against Murdoch. And if she had such an opportunity in mind, then it would explain the freedom with which she had talked of them. I did not reject the premise that she and Brunning were intimates, but I did admit that the matter was in doubt.

'You appear then to know much of what I was to tell you of Murdoch,' I said. 'What you do not know you can learn from the Fräulein. We are travelling to Vichy, and our task there will not be easy, particularly since Murdoch and Dell are acquainted with some of our plans.'

'I am distressed by that,' said Brunning.

'You are not alone,' I retorted. 'There is a leakage—it is through von Stroem. I propose to arrange for you to work with von Stroem. You will endeavour to find what weakness the man has—he has some, of that I am sure. I think it may be women.'

51

Brunning looked a little disappointed, but his answer was prompt.

'I will do my best, Excellency.'

'It is what I should expect.' I went into some detail about the methods he was to adopt when we reached Vichy, and dismissed him. I did not delay then in telephoning Paris, where the headquarters of my French organisation was established. This organisation, now controlled by one of Goering's protégés, had been completely successful at the time when I left France for England; I had not expected to return to it, but through Elsa I had maintained all the records, and had arranged to have forwarded to me duplicates of all documents concerning the French occupation. Some of these had been unsatisfactory. There was less unrest in the towns than in the country, but there was too much in both.

Prisoners of war can prove admirable hostages, particularly where their native country is under foreign rule.

Schlesser, in Paris, had already been advised that I would be operating. Everything would be put at my disposal, he assured me.

I felt more satisfied.

After all, the efforts of the woman Dell and of Angell and Fuller were of little importance. In fact only their knowledge of what was about to happen need be disconcerting, and it would not take long to discover how they contrived to learn it. Their absurd and theatrical antics with the letter, the card in the car, and the aeroplane were clearly calculated to harrass and disturb me; they would soon learn that there was nothing to be obtained by such childish methods.

Brunning reported at last that the aeroplane had arrived. Fritz and Joachim assisted me to my chair, and I was wheeled to the 'plane. There were no bright lights, but enough to see by a crescent moon. It was with considerable effort that I was manœuvred into the cabin, but I glanced round the interior with approval. One seat had been removed, and a long-chair put in its place, so that I could stretch my leg straight out in its most comfortable position.

Joachim took the controls: he is an expert pilot as well

as a first-class chauffeur-mechanic, and because of the possibility that I would need him to take me long distances, he made a weekly flight in order to keep in practice. When Brunning had settled in beside me and Fritz had called his farewell, Joachim eased back on the stick, and the twin-engines roared as he widened the throttle. It was a perfect take-off—my mood of satisfaction deepened. I should be in Vichy before daylight, and would then be able to sleep as well in the cabin as in my bed. The droning of the engines lulled me into a state of pleasant drowsiness, and I did not try to stir myself to great mental effort.

My task was to find Mondel. I had to make sure he was presented to the Leader (or the Leader's representative) and success would prove my ability beyond all question. I did not think it would be long before I solved von Stroem's second problem, that of finding Murdoch and Dell. But I must make sure von Stroem had to give me the full credit. I was living again, and I meant to continue living.

I do not know when I dropped off to sleep.

I remember the touch of a hand on my arm, and waking in complete darkness. There had been a faint blue light in the cabin before.

I heard Brunning's hard breathing.

'What is it?' I demanded, and because I had been awakened so suddenly I could not avoid a momentary feeling of trepidation.

He did not immediately reply.

'What is it?' I rasped.

'Your pardon, Excellency,' said Brunning, and I heard a clicking sound, then realised that he was taking earphones from his head. 'We are being followed,' he stated quietly.

'Followed? In the air? That is absurd!'

'I thought it was,' said Brunning, 'but it is so, Excellency. I have just radioed for a fighter escort.'

I was not deeply alarmed but could no longer sleep, and I waited with Brunning and Joachim as the latter sent the Dornier through the black heavens, tense and expectant. The moon had waned; there was nothing about us but the black void, above us the stars—and behind us another aircraft: a hostile one.

Fighter Escort

In the air a man is more aware of his dependence on others than in any other circumstance. A ship can be sailed without its captain, the driver of a train can be changed, in a car there is the security of the earth and familiar landmarks about one. It is less obvious that one man, another man, temporarily controls one's destiny.

I was more aware of Joachim's broad back than of Brunning at my side, although I knew that in an emergency Brunning would be able to take over the controls. I have much faith in him, but little in his ability to pilot an aircraft. I preferred conversation to the silence, which seemed in one way more profound because of the drone of the engine.

'Joachim,' I called. 'At what height are we flying?'

'Six thousand feet, Excellency.'

'Have you radioed for the weather reports?'

'They are satisfactory,' said Joachim.

'How long have we been followed?'

'It is eleven minutes since I became aware of it, Excellency,' he said.

'What warned you of it?'

'A light reflected in the mirror,' answered Joachim, indicating the long mirror-panel above his head. 'It was the striking of a match, and no one should strike matches in an aeroplane. No member of the *Luftwaffe* would do so.'

'It is the kind of madness which an Englishman would indulge.'

'I had considered that, Excellency.'

'At what speed are we travelling?'

'One hundred and eighty-three miles an hour,' answered Joachim. 'We were cruising at two hundred and nine when I sighted the light and I increased to two hundred and forty-one.' His precision of detail was very much in evidence. 'I immediately put into operation the sound indicator, and ensured that a machine was behind us. It's speed increased with ours, and later decreased. I slowed down in order to enable the fighter escort to reach us more quickly.'

'That is good,' I said.

I thought of a fool who would strike a match in an aeroplane—Angell or Fuller, perhaps, or even Mary Dell. Fuller especially might wish to smoke. It was an uncomfortable thought that they were behind me, although I did not seriously doubt their identity.

After the shooting in the grounds of my house it seemed at least possible that they would wish to crash this aeroplane, but I had faith enough in Joachim's ability to avoid such a disaster. There was, however, the possibility that they were following simply to find out where I was going. They would surely not risk an action in the air when they could so easily be attacked by ground defences as well as by night-fighters.

'Brunning, radio again to the ground,' I ordered. 'Inform the escort that the machine behind us is to be traced and that its occupants are to be apprehended once they land.'

Brunning demurred, a thing he does not usually do.

'Is it wise, Excellency? Messages can be detected by any radio the others are carrying.'

'They are already warned that we have sent for assistance,' I told him sharply. 'Proceed.'

'At once, Excellency.' I heard him speaking in a low voice into the transmitting set. After a pause he turned back to me. 'The order has been received on the ground, and is being remitted to the escort which is already on the way.'

'Good,' I said, and relapsed again into silence.

I was annoyed that Brunning had questioned my order. I do not claim to be immune from mistakes, but any decision I make is made after considerable thought. For some reason which I could not fully understand, that moment made me think again of the possibility of a liaison between Brunning and Elsa. It displeased me even more than it had done before, but again there was no moment for discussing it. In any case, I needed Brunning to operate with von Stroem, and I did not wish to say anything which might jeopardise his judgment; anxiety over a woman is the most likely thing to do that.

55

I thought of Elsa and von Stroem.

Had he realised that she had followed him? If so, had she successfully explained a reason which would not arouse his suspicions? I was worried lest, for once, she had failed. She had not been herself since the receipt of the letter from Mary Dell. I began to feel enraged by all the things that had gone wrong. Here was I on the threshold of a triumph which would resound through the Party. Fools who had declared that Ludvic von Horssell was finished, an old man of no further use to the Fatherland, would change their tone. I would again wield the power which I had done for so many years.

But from the moment von Stroem had arrived there had been trouble and difficulty. Even the accursed old woman begging for pfennigs and screaming oaths at me, had brought an interruption which had forced my mind from the main issue. But that was incidental. Murdoch and Dell were to blame.

It was a bleak period of reflection.

My resistance to outside influences was then at its lowest, and I grew more depressed perhaps than the circumstances justified. But I was cheered up shortly afterwards, for after the warning signal on the receiving set had echoed through the cabin, and after listening for a moment, Brunning turned to me.

'The escort of three Messerschmitts is with us, Excellency.'

'And they understand what they are to do?'

'In the event of the following 'plane leaving us, Excellency, one fighter is to follow it, and the others to continue with us for the rest of the journey.'

'That is satisfactory,' I declared.

I thought then for the first time of the moment when von Stroem had told me that if I were followed, I should make arrangements to find out who was in my wake. I had told him it was an elementary precaution, but had not thought at the time of the possibility of being followed in the air. I brooded, then decided how I should discuss the matter with von Stroem. I would tell him that I had deliberately started out on my own, in order to encourage Fuller or Dell, or whoever was behind me, to keep close. That done, I had sent for the escort.

Perhaps ten minutes passed before I asked Joachim:
'What does your sound indicator tell you?'

'I believe that I can detect the note of the Dornier that was behind us as well as the escort 'planes, Excellency, but it is difficult to be sure.'

'We shall arrive safely,' Brunning interposed.

'Of course we shall arrive safely! I said sharply. 'I had not doubted it.'

In the silence that followed the eeriness of the situation seemed greater. Four 'planes were about us, all moving at high speed through the void, and in one of them were Murdoch's agents. I was the more amazed by their daring as I dwelt on that. Enough that they had contrived to be in the grounds of my house, enough that they had contrived to be in Vienna; but to have an aeroplane, to be able to fuel it and to take-off from a German or an Austrian airfield, and to dare to follow me in the air—that was too much.

Another thought entered my mind. Angell and Fuller had been working in the grounds of my house for two weeks or more. They had served long enough to ingratiate themselves with Lieber and the other guards. Yet surely von Stroem had not planned his visit to me as far back as that?

They had prepared to work against me two weeks before anyone could have known with certainty that I was likely to come out of retirement.

For some seconds I did not breathe easily, and the constriction in my throat threatened to choke me. Joachim turned his head, while Brunning leaned forward and rested a hand on my shoulder.

'You are not well, Excellency?'

'Ach, it is nothing,' I said, and he took his hand away.

My breathing grew easier, and I was able to consider that new realisation with detachment. How could Murdoch possibly have realised that I was to operate again before von Stroem had named me? von Stroem had inferred that he had not thought of me until the problem of Mondel had arisen.

It was growing clear that von Stroem had been planning to invite my co-operation for some time past, and had confided that much in someone whom he believed he could trust but who had betrayed him. My anger was less with the betrayer than with von Stroem. It was intolerable that he should tell me only half-truths.

As we droned through the air, my thoughts grew clearer. As I have said, I do not doubt that von Stroem planned to capitalise on my success. Until that moment I had not thought of doing more than obtaining a full acknowledgement of my services for myself. But if von Stroem was planning to twist the facts to his own advantage, why should I not do the same?

He had called himself a 'man of mystery'; and he had a reputation for absolute efficiency. Now, however, I had reasonable evidence that he had allowed vital information to leak out. Once the Leader learned of that he would have no time for von Stroem; his executive officers must be reliable in every way.

I will not discuss this with you when we reach Vichy, I thought. I shall collect more evidence of your negligence, and I shall allow you to believe that I do not realise it. I think perhaps you will be less of a man of mystery and efficiency when my full report is made to Berchtesgarten.

I smiled to myself in the darkness of the cabin. I actually forgot the mysterious aeroplane behind us until, abruptly, there was a vivid flash outside.

It came through the utter darkness without warning. It illuminated every inch of the cabin, showing Brunning, opposite me and leaning back against a cushion at his head. The light had awakened him fully, and he looked comical, with his head tilted back and wide nostrils showing like black voids. The light, which had a blueish hue, showed Joachim, half-turning in his seat.

It also illuminated the space beyond the cabin, and four aeroplanes flying within a mile of the Dornier; yes, it was as wide and extensive as that! I recognised three Messerschmitts and one Dornier, like mine, and could even see the heads and shoulders of the people in the cabin. There was a man and a woman, and I did not doubt that it was Angell or Fuller, and Mary Dell.

But the blue light was more powerful even than that.

It revealed the ground beneath.

58

It showed a railway junction and every building in a town over which we were flying. For miles around, even to the fields and scattered buildings of the countryside about the town, the light spread its brilliance. It was as if the night had suddenly been transformed to day.

'What is it?' Brunning gasped.

Suddenly I realised exactly what it was, for I saw flashes of yellow flame below us—flashes that could only come from anti-aircraft fire. Almost immediately after, bursts of fire showed in the heavens, perhaps two miles to the right of the cabin. The brilliant blue light faded, and I could see little, although I could guess what would have been visible had the light lasted a little longer.

'It is the American flash-bomb!' I said. 'Have you not the sense to understand that?'

'The flash-bomb!' exclaimed Brunning.

'The British have it and are taking night photographs,' said Joachim, without turning, but he had immediately swung his stick so that we flew away from the exploding shells. I wondered fleetingly whether even this precaution could protect us from danger, for the gunfire appeared to be coming nearer. One solitary night reconnaissance 'plane from England might have aroused the activity; or the flash-bomb might be to help a flight of bombers about to raid the town. That would mean that the whole night sky would be alive with shrapnel.

9

At Vichy

I have done little night flying over hostile country, and only once before had I been within seeing distance of anti-aircraft fire. I have been bombed, although usually when I have been quite safe, and in any case it is different; there are those who say that the chances of being hit while in the air are infinitely less than of being injured by bombs or bomb-splinters while on the ground, but I cannot subscribe to that opinion. Certainly for the next five minutes I was in a state of constant tension.

Shells burst all around us.

Sometimes they were illuminating enough for me to see some of the escort of fighters, which had separated; they offered no protection now.

The barrage from the ground was an astonishing sight; moreover, searchlights of many colours were directed towards the heavens and once or twice I caught a glimpse of a machine vivid in orange or blue or yellow. Once, too, a concentration of such lights gathered just ahead of my craft, but Joachim turned the machine away abruptly. It made me slide in my seat uncomfortably, but I did not object to that; it was unavoidable and necessary.

The ground more than the sky was a blaze of light.

I was startled to find that the concentrated fire from the guns, from some slow-moving lights—called colloquially, I believe, flaming onions—and the searchlights illuminated the town so clearly. Hitherto I had thought that the science of defending the country against night bombing was well advanced; the English, with their conservatism, did not shed so much light about the skies.

I now knew why.

The sky was aglow, and the aeroplanes more easily visible; but so was the earth, and the bombers' targets.

I saw bombs exploding.

I was fascinated, although I was cursing the British bombers. They sight with incredible accuracy, and it is almost impossible to believe the truth: that they will fly in and out of such a barrage continuously for half an hour or more to ensure a good run to their target. I have no room for lies, as such; it is not true that the British deliberately bomb the residential parts of towns. Bombs fall on those quarters it is true, but that is inevitable; ours do also. They have successfully postponed the hour of their inevitable defeat by concentrating on military objectives, particularly the synthetic oil plants and refineries for that life-blood of modern warfare. This increased our difficulties ten-fold; and that night they were attacking a railway station and a marshalling yard. I saw the bombs bursting on the glistening rails with awful regularity; here and there some fell to one side, but for the most part they were on or near their objective. I saw one immense bomber swoop so low that from the height which I was flying—Joachim had begun to climb immediately the shooting started—that it seemed to skim the tops of a great church before unloading a stick of bombs across the station itself.

Fires were already starting.

They had showered incendiaries, of course, and although many flickered out, some started huge fires which sent flames hundreds of feet into the air. Suddenly I saw an explosion even greater than anything which had preceded it, and I heard Brunning mutter:

'The swine! They have hit an ammunition train.'

I saw the train, a long line of trucks and carriages, and explosion after explosion burst from it, hurling flame and debris over an ever-increasing area. Below me, in fact, that part of the town was an inferno.

I was sick at the thought of so much damage.

But Joachim was taking me away from the town, and slowly it dropped behind us, although the fires could still be clearly seen, as well as the bursting A.A. shells some miles in our rear. I saw also that two of the fighter 'planes and the other Dornier were with us; the silhouettes of the machines showed against the lurid glow.

One of the fighters was missing.

'Did you see what happened to it?' I asked Brunning.

He had not, but Joachim said:

'It received a direct hit, Excellency, and disintegrated in mid-air.'

I nodded, and asked: 'What city was attacked?'

'That was Munich, Excellency.'

It was not the first time that the British had been as far as Munich, but I could not keep out of my mind some degree of admiration for the crews which flew their aeroplanes such vast distances, and even then hovered over their target long enough to get the most effect out of every bomb. I hate the English as a Christian hates the Devil, but they have great courage. And they fight as no other race on earth, my own not excepted.

'We were fortunate,' remarked Brunning.

61

'Is there the need for such obvious comments?' I asked irritably. 'We were lucky to see the defences in action at such a peak. If you imply we were lucky to escape, you should know that it is no more than one chance in fifty that we should receive damage while in the air.'

'Of course, Excellency,' said Brunning.

Munich was a long way behind us, and only two of the fires could be seen, when next there was an interruption. I was dozing again when awakened by the stutter of machine-gun fire. I opened my eyes to see tracer bullets passing—just outside my window!

I saw quickly, also, that it was not the Dornier which was being attacked, but one of the fighters. I could not see the assailant, but Brunning muttered:

'One of those accursed bombers, on its way back!'

'It is likely,' I admitted.

There was a cross-fire of shooting, from which Joachim veered swiftly, and the tracers went further away. But suddenly I saw a sight as terrible as I am likely to see in my life.

An aircraft exploded in mid-air.

I had seen one stream of tracer bullets falling downwards and eventually going out of sight, and the other stopping abruptly, and starting small fires—or what seemed to be fires—in the cockpit of one of the machines. Abruptly there came the flash only a split-second before the roar, which could be clearly heard. My aircraft reared over on its side, as if out of control.

There was the one blinding flash from the doomed machine, which then began to fall in two main pieces. Burning debris also fell, a hundred beacons of light dropping towards the earth.

Joachim for once spoke out of his turn.

'We have but one escort left,' he stated.

'We shall have no more trouble,' Brunning asserted.

I regarded him coldly, although, of course, in the darkness he was not aware of that. I wrestled with myself, trying to decide whether to make any comment or not. I knew that I was prejudiced against him; his possible relationship with Elsa was the reason for that.

'Is the Dornier still with us?' I asked Joachim.

'Yes, Excellency.'

I was perturbed; the machine had escaped as lightly as we, and had not taken the opportunity of getting away while the fighters had been too busy to follow it.

There was nothing I could do, and at least it seemed as if one fear was gone—the fear that the Dornier proposed to attack us. Had it wished to, it could have done so much earlier, particularly during the fight over Munich.

I was surprised that the details of that attack should fade so easily from my mind.

At the moment when I had seen the train exploding carriage by carriage I had been sick at heart, but now it seemed unimportant. Perhaps that was because I knew that it would not be long before we were flying over the occupied territory of France. For how many years I have longed to have France beneath the heel! That accursed nation, so often defeated and yet so often re-gathering its strength to defy the Fatherland again, had to be crushed once and for all. Let the politicians talk of 'honourable settlement' if they wish. This time there must not be the fatal mistake of 1871, when Paris was occupied and when France could have become a German colony. Bismarck threw that opportunity away; not of his own accord, but because politicians fooled him into the mistake.

The Führer will not make the same mistake. France will never live as a separate entity again.

As these thoughts passed through my mind there was silence and peace about us.

It was difficult to believe that we had flown through such a holocaust of fire and shrapnel and escaped without damage, but we had, and I was reassured. I did not feel like sleeping, and told Brunning to pour me out some coffee from the Thermos flask. He did so, and the hot beverage —practically the only one that I can drink in normal times —warmed and comforted me.

'How far have we to go?' I asked Joachim.

'We shall be there in little more than an hour and a half, Excellency,' he said. 'It has been a good flight.'

I stared at his unmoving back.

'A good flight!' I roared. 'Ho-ho-ho! You have a sense of humour, Joachim, I did not know it! A good flight, indeed! As peaceful a journey as a babe at his mothers' breast, eh Joachim?'

'Except that we have been more conscious of danger, yes, Excellency,' said Joachim. 'We have made good time.'

The man was serious, after all.

I smoked a cigarette after that, for the machine—as are all of those in which I fly—was specially protected so that smoking is safe. I knew that Brunning wished to smoke, but did not give him permission. Had I done so I believe he would have reminded me of my comment about the match which had first told Joachim we were being followed.

Three 'planes, then, flew one after the other through the darkness. It did not seem half an hour when Brunning touched my shoulder, and said quietly:

'We are landing, Excellency.'

It was still dark, but not far below I could see the flares of a landing-field—such flares were safe enough in France. I knew the 'plane was no more than a thousand feet up, circling for the final straight run into the wind. I thought immediately of the other 'planes, but it was not a moment for me to ask Joachim questions.

Suddenly he exclaimed: 'Excellency! It is unbelievable!'

'What is?' I snapped.

'The Dornier, Excellency—it also prepares to land!'

He could not turn in his seat, and consequently I had to stare at his back. I could scarcely credit the truth of what he was saying. The other aircraft was going to land with us or before us.

Before us!

I saw its dark shape cross one of the landing-lights, and a few seconds later saw it taxi-ing across the landing-field. I saw the little shapes of mechanics running towards it, but was too amazed to think.

Joachim said in a strained voice: 'We are about to land, Excellency.'

That gave me time to protect my right side against any jolt which might be forthcoming, but he landed smoothly, and it was difficult to detect the actual moment when we reached *terra firma*. There were many lights about us—too many, I thought, although that was because I had been so

64

long in countries where the blackout had been rigidly enforced.

Figures appeared at the cabin window.

The door opened—and then I saw the man and the woman from the other 'plane, and I could have cursed myself for not suspecting it before.

The woman was Elsa: the man was von Stroem.

10

Unexpected Meeting

Certainly it would have been useless to reveal the anger I felt. I have always maintained an expressionless face, and have never regretted that I have acquired the habit; it has enabled me to overcome more awkward moments even than this.

I sat back at ease in the special seat.

'So,' I said, 'we arrive together, Herr Baron.'

'I hurried to assure myself that you were not hurt,' said von Stroem, but I believed the man was lying—he had come to gloat over me. I made that clear immediately.

'It might perhaps have been better had you told me that you would be flying so close to me,' I said, 'instead of alarming my crew. While I was sleeping they sent for the escort.'

'That was as well,' said von Stroem drily. 'Had we encountered the bombers over Munich without an escort, either my 'plane or yours would have crashed. We can congratulate each other. You have made the journey without undue fatigue, I trust.'

'I shall need no more rest,' I said.

'You are fortunate,' said von Stroem 'I will confess that I have not slept well. The Fräulein, however, has slept most of the way.'

'We accustom ourselves to sleeping where we can,' I said.

von Stroem bowed, and then a man arrived from a car

which had drawn up alongside my 'plane. It was the special car with the long-seat which I had earlier ordered by telephone. I was helped from the cabin, and with the aid of my stick reached the car. The ground was damp, and once my stick stuck in mud; I thought I would fall, but Joachim's hand was on my arm, and he steadied me.

'Is there anything you wish to discuss tonight?' I asked von Stroem, for whom another car had drawn up.

'No, Excellency, but I shall present myself by ten o'clock in the morning. The Fräulein is good enough to tell me that you are staying at *l'Hôtel Grande*, using, officially, the name of Horst.'

'It is so,' I said, for some measure of anonymity is wise.

'And as she knows, I am staying at *l'Hôtel Berliner*,' declared von Stroem. I could have sworn that there was a sardonic smile on his lips, and it seemed to be as if by his choice of hotel he was impuning my loyalty. But I nodded and smiled as I stepped with difficulty into the car, and stretched my leg out so that it went the full length of the body—the seat next to the driver's being removed and a stool replacing it.

Where it is avoidable, I will not allow myself to be driven by any man but Joachim, and he took the place of the chauffeur who had brought the car. Brunning and another man climbed into my second car. I allowed von Stroem to go ahead in his, then called to Brunning.

He hurried to me.

'You have your opportunity,' I said 'He will be at *l'Hôtel Berliner* for the rest of the night. You should have a chance to make him realise that he is not safe on his own. I shall leave the execution of the plan to you.'

'It shall be done, Excellency,' said Brunning quickly, and I know the man was pleased at the trust I imposed in him.

'His suite is on the first floor,' Elsa said quietly, 'entered by doors 18 and 20.'

'A thousand thanks, Fräulein!' Brunning turned hurriedly, and the car moved off before mine. Some distance ahead, and at the gates of the airfield, the rear light of von Stroem's car showed. Brunning would catch up with him, perhaps even be at the hotel ahead of him.

But Elsa had to explain how she had come to be with

von Stroem. It would not be true to say that I was displeased, for his manner had not suggested that he suspected that I had set her the task of following him; but I would not easily overlook the needless anxiety I had suffered in the air.

She settled down in her seat, and said:

'Will a cigarette worry you, Ludvic?'

I was surprised at the 'Ludvic'. True, we were in the close proximity in which we often travelled, and there was no need for her to be so formal when we were out of the office. Moreover the glass partition was closed, and Joachim could hear nothing in the front.

'No,' I said. 'You may smoke—again.'

She stared at me in surprise.

'Again? What do you mean?'

'You were smoking in the cabin—that is how I detected you in the air.'

'That is not so,' she said promptly, and then paused to light her cigarette. It glowed very red in the darkness of the car. 'There was no smoking. von Stroem would not permit it.'

'A match was struck,' I insisted.

'Not even that,' said Elsa. 'I pretended to sleep part of the way, but actually I was fully awake. I would have known had that happened.'

A momentary spasm of disquiet seized me, but it soon passed.

'There was such a light,' I declared. 'Joachim also saw it. It was immediately after that that the escort was sent for.'

'It was not from our machine,' Elsa asseverated.

The spasm of alarm came again, more sharply.

'If that is true, then there was a light from another machine before the Messerschmitts arrived,' I said. 'Could it be that we were both followed? Did you know of another aircraft?'

'Other than yours, no,' said Elsa, and she too was aware of tension. 'Could Murdoch . . .'

I leaned back in my seat.

'That accursed man!' I exclaimed. 'Yes, he could have had a machine behind us, and Joachim, while detecting the note of one engine, could not be sure of two.'

I disliked the discovery, but there was nothing to be done about it now; it was useless to arrange for a search 'plane to go up during the hours of darkness, and as the engine had certainly been of German manufacture there was little likelihood that its movements had been traced by sound detectors from the ground.

How I cursed von Stroem!

Had it not amused him to follow me so closely I would have been in a much better position, and the pursuit machine would have been followed. As it was, von Stroem's little trick had destroyed the usefulness of the fighter escort.

'The time will come when the dear Baron will find his jokes miscarrying badly,' I said gruffly. 'What did you learn of him, Elsa? And how did it come that you travelled with him?'

For a moment the glowing end of her cigarette illuminated her face. She was looking at me, and the red glow shone on her amber eyes, making them seem very large and beautiful. She took the cigarette from her lips and crushed it in the tray at the side of the car.

'I followed him until he went into the Gestapo Headquarters,' she told me. 'There I took a taxi, for the Mercedes was too conspicuous.'

I nodded my approval.

'He was in the building for perhaps half an hour,' went on Elsa, 'then came out hurriedly, and on his own. My taxi driver did well, and followed him to the Libstrassa Hotel.'

'Yes,' I said, when she paused.

'It was not difficult, with my pass, to locate his room, and to learn what there was to learn about him.' Elsa spoke as if she had made discoveries of considerable importance. I leaned forward, hopeful and expectant. 'I did not question the S.S. men on duty in the foyer since I believed they would report any questions to him. I was able to ensure information and discretion from the assistant manager of the hotel—Halle, you know of him.'

'He is reliable, yes.'

'Halle was curiously eager to talk,' said Elsa. 'He had received orders a week before for the rooms to be prepared for von Stroem, but not until five days after the reservation did von Stroem arrive. With him was an official known to be employed at Berchtesgarten.'

'That is not surprising,' I said.

'No. The official stayed only a few hours, but von Stroem had reserved three rooms. It is remarkable,' added Elsa slowly, 'that officially they were not occupied, although the beds were slept in.'

My neck and throat began to contract.

'Yes?' The word came thinly from my lips.

'By women,' said Elsa, and she laughed very softly. 'He has done well, Ludvic: few people suspect that he is interested in women, he is reputedly a misogynist. But these are facts,' she said, 'supported by the words of two chamber-maids and a waiter. No meals were served, and officially the women did not stay at the hotel—but they shared the apartment with von Stroem.'

I began to laugh, deep in my throat.

'Two,' I said. 'Two, in one night! Truly a man of unsuspected attractiveness and powers. Elsa! Did *you* find that he was easily impressed?'

She turned towards me; I could not see her but I knew that she was smiling.

'He is most amorous,' she declared.

'Even in the aeroplane cabin!' I exclaimed, and I began to shake with laughter; it was good to laugh, and even better to know that von Stroem had this unsuspected and unconfessed weakness. At the back of my mind was the dark thought that he may have talked carelessly to a woman, and that thus word had leaked through to Murdoch. He . . .

I stopped laughing abruptly, and stared through the gloom. I felt my heart beating faster, and I gripped the arm of my seat.

'Elsa!' I snapped. 'Do you realise what this could mean?'

'In what way, Excellency?'

There is little doubt that she did know, but she deferred to me, and I went on softly:

'One of the women could have been Mary Dell!'

'It is just conceivable,' admitted Elsa.

I snapped: 'Were they of the streets?'

'Yes. One was well known to Halle—a beauty, and expensive. The other was not known, but there is doubt as to whether she could be Dell.'

'What doubt?'

'She was dark.'

'Dell *is* dark!' I snapped, but then I stopped, for I realised that the woman seen in the car outside the walls of my house had been fair; there was a note in the book in my pocket to tell Elsa that Mary Dell had almost certainly dyed her hair.

'Yes,' said Elsa slowly, 'but she would not be likely to remain dark while in Austria or Germany.'

'No,' I admitted. 'So one woman was a familiar of Halle's, the stranger was dark-haired. Could you get no description of her?'

'None,' replied Elsa. 'None, except that she was beautiful, and . . .' She hesitated a moment, and I wondered why until she added very softly: 'Halle believes her to be a Jewess, Excellency.'

'A Jewess!'

Little wonder that I exclaimed, little wonder that the information seemed of greater importance than the fact that such a description made it virtually impossible for the woman to be Mary Dell. I was less interested then in the possibility that von Stroem had been fool enough to allow Murdoch's strongest agent to share his bed. (Nor at the time did I remember that such an eventuality was most unlikely. The English seldom give themselves utterly to their country, which is one of the reasons why their espionage is so seriously lacking in the essential woman factor. Murdoch's wife would not become intimate with any man, no matter what the price; but as I say, I overlooked that psychological fact while the thoughts flashed through my mind.)

von Stroem, associating with a Jewess!

Small wonder Halle, a conscientious manager and one with a zealous hatred of the Jewish race, had been 'curiously eager to talk'!

And it explained so much.

There is no Jew in the world faithful to the Nazi ideals; it would be folly to imagine such faithfulness possible. Even without the Nuremberg Laws and the righteous persecution of a race which had polluted every country with which it had contacted, and has explained the gradual deterioration of the Aryan race through the centuries, I would not have trusted a Jew. I do not hate them; I despise them, I am revolted by them.

von Stroem, then, had a secret mistress, a Jewess who would be only too eager to dispense information to Murdoch and Dell. This was information which would ensure that von Stroem was dismissed from his post. More likely he would be executed.

How well the man was playing into my hands!

But I knew that I must not allow the personal angle to be too prominent. Mondel and the meeting with the Führer came first; once I had successfully accomplished my purpose I could deal with von Stroem.

'A Jewess,' said Elsa, echoing my exclamation. 'I can see that you think much as I do, Excellency. There is the leakage; we must find this woman, and make sure that she is not able to send messages again. I do not think,' she added quietly, 'that it need be long.'

'No? And why?'

She laughed a little; had it been light I know that I would have seen her glistening tongue showing between her teeth; she often laughs like that, and it makes her damnably desirable. I wished to place my hand about her, but I would not.

'In the cabin, von Stroem gave me the impression that he would like a change of amusement, and I made it clear that I was not averse to his company.' She laughed again. 'You will replace von Stroem within a month, Ludvic, I am sure of that.'

I clasped her thigh with my left hand.

'It is so, Elsa! And I shall not forget your thought.'

'I have not yet finished,' Elsa said. 'After making the inquiries, I returned for my car, then drove in it to the hotel. I wished to make it impossible for a report to reach von Stroem that I had been there, without safeguarding myself. I called at his rooms. He received me courteously. I apologised for interrupting, but told him that there were details about Lirchner—his man who was killed in a car accident —which you felt it wise to know. He agreed, and after he had talked, giving me information which in any case I possessed, it was too late for me to return—or I thought it was. He suggested that I should fly with him, and, of course, I agreed.' She laughed again. 'At the airport, we learned you had been delayed because of engine trouble with your aircraft.'

'Engine trouble!' I exclaimed, and went more fully into the details. Her pleasure at her own discoveries faded; she was anxious and concerned, and I knew her chief concern was a personal one for me. I warmed towards her, and talked disparagingly of the effort of Angell and Fuller. She grew more satisfied, while it was not long before we drew up outside the hotel. A long-chair was waiting for me; Joachim wheeled me to the lift, and to the first-floor suite which I had arranged to have. Joachim opened the door, I motioned Elsa through, and then Joachim pushed me into the room.

And then abruptly the door was closed by a man standing behind it. I turned my head, and I saw myself looking into the face of Michael Fuller, whom I believed to be in the air even at that moment.

Murdoch's man was waiting for me here!

11

I am Threatened

Fuller held an automatic in front of him, and on it was the ugly snout of a silencer. I had not the slightest doubt that if I or any of the others made any attempt to summon help, he would fire. But that was not the thing which was primarily on my mind.

He had not fired immediately. He did not wish to kill me. So he wanted information.

He was not likely to get it, although as I stared at him I prepared a rigmarole which might serve a useful purpose. I was wondering how to get him out of the room without danger to any of us, especially to Elsa and to me. Joachim would seize the faintest opportunity for action, but Fuller was in some ways as elusive as Murdoch.

None of these things I have mentioned were the most important things in my mind. That was a very simple and obvious fact—something which Elsa and Joachim could see as easily as I: *Fuller was not disguised.* I think I have mentioned that he is a man of medium height, broad-shouldered and rather stocky. He has untidy brown hair, and a fresh complexion. His features have that attractive kind of English ugliness: the man would be popular amongst English women.

The lack of disguise puzzled me more than anything else.

And Fuller spoke in English, smilingly. They are always smiling, these English agents—to them it appears that the most sacred cause is a joke.

'Why, why!' he exclaimed. 'Aren't you so well, Baron? I thought you were at your hale and hearty best in Vienna.'

I would gladly have strangled him.

von Stroem's evasive references to my infirmity had been bad enough, but this direct thrust, a cheap gibe which no man needed to make, infuriated me. I do not think I showed it. I once told Murdoch that if he mentioned it again I would cut his throat—at a time when I could have done so.

'In Vienna,' I said, 'I was preparing for you and Murdoch.'

'Oh, jolly nice thought,' said the idiot. 'Y'know, Baron, in a more peaceful world I believe you could be quite a hospitable chap.'

'When the peace of the New Order is fully established,' I said, 'you will not be alive to know it.'

'If there's to be a Nazi New Order, I'm for the Suicide Squad,' he said lightly. 'But there isn't, Baron. After all, forty million Frenchmen can't be wrong.'

'Wrong in what?' asked Elsa.

'In what?' mimicked Fuller. 'My dear sweet Elsa, in France of course. Under the German heel, don't they say so in the Press? The French don't like their sample of the New Order. And,' he added, leaning back against the wall and talking for all the world as if he had as much time as he wanted for talking, 'I have heard it said that there are

73

others who don't like it. The Dutch, the Belgians, the Danes, the Norwegians, the . . .'

'That is enough nonsense,' snapped Elsa, whose command of his English is excellent. 'You did not come here to waste words.'

'Too true,' agreed Fuller. 'I came to deliver an ultimatum. One might say an Awful Warning.' He had the audacity to laugh! 'Actually I think we've done pretty well today. Mary's *billet doux* must have turned you over quite a bit, my pet, and what with the unfortunate accident to the aeroplane, the spot of bother over Munich, and this that and the other, you must have been warned pretty well as it is.'

'What are you talking about?' demanded Elsa.

I thought: so he was behind us over Munich. He landed somewhere near here. He must have had French assistance, of course—some accursed French people were always prepared to help the English. But I was greatly perturbed by the ease and the speed of his movements.

'I'm talking about this,' said Fuller, and his voice hardened. 'You two once retired, and it will be wise of you to stay that way. The Baron's not fit for active service.'

I glared at him.

'You will see whether I am able to work!'

'You were always a talkative fool,' said Elsa in a tone calculated to sting him to some retort which might betray information of importance.

'Yes, wasn't I?' asked Fuller. 'But it's hardly fair to keep you in suspense. The warning is only part of the object of the visit. The other is . . .' He hesitated, and then smiled at us, raising one eyebrow over the other. 'But perhaps I won't commit myself. Bruce wouldn't like it.'

His gun was held a little less carefully, and already in my mind there was an idea by which he could be outwitted. The wheel chair was electrically driven, although Joachim had pushed it from the street. It would not be difficult to switch on the current, and move it in reverse, after releasing the brakes. A movement forward would bring a shot; a movement *backwards* would startle Fuller, and give Joachim the chance to draw his gun.

Elsa said in a low-pitched voice: 'So Murdoch is here.'

'Hadn't you guessed?' asked Fuller. 'He is always where you least expect him. He controls operations far more effectively than you ever could, my dear Baron.' It was a clumsy attempt at mockery, and it failed completely, particularly since I was so immersed in the problem of switching on the current without making it too obvious. I played with the switch, which is easy to hand, but before I had pressed it, footsteps sounded outside.

Fuller stiffened, but did not glance towards the door.

'Keep quite still, all of you,' he ordered.

He had not moved from his position behind the door, but he would not have an easy task to deal with anyone else who entered. I was preparing to say 'come in' to whoever knocked, relying on my belief that Fuller did not then wish to kill me, when the door opened without a knock.

I saw Joachim's right hand twitch, a positive indication that he was ready to take the slightest opportunity which might be offered, and I saw him glance towards the door.

His hand did not move further.

I turned my head, and I was as astounded as he—and as Elsa, for that matter. I do not think that any one of us could have taken advantage of any false move on Fuller's part had he made one. For we saw a woman of arresting beauty.

In fact not for some minutes did I realise she was a Jewess.

I should have done, from her slightly large nose; I might have guessed from her full lips, which parted in surprise when she saw me. I could have judged from her raven black hair, from her bold, brown eyes. But the first thing I noticed of that woman was her exceptional beauty.

She paused on the threshold.

'Come in,' said Fuller, speaking in French, and as if against her will she entered. Fuller kicked the door to, but there was a faint contraction of the muscles of his cheeks. *He recognised the intruder*.

She stared at him, and at the gun in his hand.

'What—what is happening, please?' Her French was good but it had a German accent; her voice was deep and throaty. Something about her eyes as she spoke confirmed that she was one of the accursed race.

'Come right in and join the party,' said Fuller. He used idiomatic French so that it followed the English saying closely, and he was frowning at her.

'But I do not understand.' By then I felt she was acting; I believed that she knew him, and that her entry was pre-arranged, although I could not see the purpose behind it. 'I did not come to see any of you, I came to see . . .'

She stopped then.

But her lips formed the words *'Baron von . . .'*

Already I felt sure that this woman was the dark-haired beauty of whom Elsa had learned; she was the woman who was a close acquaintance of von Stroem. She had come to see him! How she could have confused the hotel with his I do not know—but then I thought that he might originally have arranged to be at *l'Hôtel Grande*, changing his decision only when he learned that I had booked there.

I did not urge her to go on, but sneered.

'Your arrival is most inopportune, madame. This gentleman is endeavouring to rob us.'

'To—*rob* you!' she exclaimed.

I could have thrashed her for her hypocrisy, yet I acknowledged to myself that she acted well.

'Oh, yes,' said Fuller, 'to rob them of their self-esteem, mademoiselle; do not be alarmed. If you would be so good as to move to the far corner of the room, and to sit with your back to me, I shall be glad.'

She did not make any comment, but turned slowly. I saw the way her dress clung to her wide hips; she had beauty of figure as well of face. Her dress was of shimmering black material, and she wore a white cape about her shoulders. Her head was bare, and she wore a pale red rose in her hair. She had been prepared for a dinner *à deux*.

She walked hesitantly.

I was wondering whether she had recognised me, and if she had what she would do. I was also thinking with satisfaction that if Fuller had not expected her—and now I do not think he had been—he was presented with an additional problem. I was already forming words with which to deceive him when he spoke again.

'Stay where you are, mam'selle!'

She stopped. I was puzzled by his sudden change of

76

orders until out of the corner of my eye I saw that she was moving her right hand upwards, beneath her left arm. I do not know whether it was deliberate; I know that Fuller thought that she was moving for a gun.

I was *fully* confident that he was not here to murder us, and with that anxiety removed from my mind, I could afford the luxury of studying his perplexity. There are advantages as well as disadvantages to being partially paralysed. Just as a blind man develops a fine sense of touch and also of hearing, so the other senses of a withered man improve. Perhaps it is because I have had no time for exercise physically that my mind has always been fully at liberty to explore. I have developed what some would call a 'sixth' sense, although it is nothing of the kind. It is the ability to reach conclusions by a swift process of thought, and to notice everything—just as I had noticed her unspoken '*Baron von . . .*'.

The woman stood quite still.

'We are now a happy little party,' said Fuller, more serious than he had spoken earlier. 'Horssell'—it pleases him and Mudoch to omit my title—'Horssell—I came here just to warn you. You won't believe it, but it is true. Go back to your little grey castle, and play with dreams. It is really all you're fit for. You once organised a Fifth Column in England. It was a puny infant compared with ours in France—and in other places.'

I wanted to scoff; and Elsa did say:

'You could always talk big!'

But I did not feel then that it was only talk. I was worried. There was the ring of truth about Fuller's statement, and I had to admit that the unrest in France was considerable, and that von Stroem had been compelled to ask my help because the problem of traitors was grievous. I believed there was much truth in what Fuller said.

'And I hope I always will talk,' went on Fuller more lightly. 'Give my regards to von Stroem, and tell him that he will meet with another accident before the night is out.'

I saw the woman start.

Fuller moved to the door and, without another word, opened it. He seemed to care nothing who was in the pas-

77

sage outside. He could move with surprising speed and stealth, and I think I was surprised when the door actually closed on him, when the moment came and he was not in the room.

It was surprising for two reasons.

One, that he should have gone with such speed and ease, leaving a sense of anti-climax. Two, that he had not tried to do anything more, but had talked in a vaguely threatening way although he must have known that I was not at all impressed.

I did not need to tell Joachim what to do.

He moved swiftly to the inner door, which connected with an ante-room, with an entry to the passage. He would try to follow Fuller, although I was not sanguine as to the outcome of his effort. I heard him go from the ante-room, which meant the second passage door was not locked, and there remained a possibility that he would find the Englishman's trail.

I could not concentrate on that. Of paramount importance was the woman in the room, the stranger whom I believed to be von Stroem's mistress. She must not know of that suspicion. Nor must she suspect that I recognised her as a Jewess, and that I hated the need for breathing in the same air as she.

She had turned, and was looking from me to Elsa in a kind of stunned surprise, as if she had been prepared for anything to happen, and that the absence of violence surprised her.

I made my voice soft.

'Mademoiselle,' I said in French, 'I regret you should have been so inconvenienced. I am sure that there is some way I can assist you. For instance, for whom were you looking?'

I did not expect her to say von Stroem, and she did not disappoint me. Her lie was of the flimsiest nature.

'My parents were here two days ago,' she said. 'I thought they would remain here. I am deeply sorry to have troubled you. And if I may now go—perhaps I can send the manager to you . . .'

She broke off, while I had to decide quickly whether to allow her to go, or whether to endeavour to make her con-

78

firm that she was looking for von Stroem. As I looked at
her I saw fear in her eyes; fear, I believed, lest she had betrayed herself.

12

Elsa has Success

The woman had betrayed herself. Had the story of expecting to find her parents here been true, there would have
been no need for 'if'. In fact she might with some excuse
have complained about the nature of her reception.

It was Elsa who broke the silence.

She is younger, she has not the same lifelong hatred of
the Jewish race which I have. My parents and their parents
before them hated the sight and sound of the Jews, with
their lisping voices and their greasy hair, their insufferable
habit of rubbing their hands together as if in anticipation
of money to be extorted. My father was never a rich man,
and in my youth I frequently resorted to moneylenders—
but never so much as I did in the months prior to the application of the Nuremberg Laws, which I knew were on the
agenda of the Party. I wrung every mark I could out of
their deep pockets. Had I not done so, others would. But
I am digressing although perhaps the knowledge that my
family has long denied Jews the right to step across their
threshold will explain in some measure the degree of my
contempt and scorn for this hybrid offshoot of the human
race.

'Allow me to telephone the manager, mam'selle,' Elsa
said in a tone which must have appeared friendly to the
other. 'I can find out where your parents have gone, and
I must do what I can to make up for your inconvenience.'

I watched the stranger narrowly, turning my head,
although Elsa saw quickly that the position was a strain,
and moved the chair so that I could watch more easily.

She hesitated, and then said in a low voice:

'Please do not worry, mam'selle. I can inquire of the manager myself.'

My stomach heaved with laughter which I was forced to repress as Elsa stepped to the telephone.

'But I insist,' she said.

The Jewess was clever; not so much as by the moving of an eyelid did she show that she was perturbed. I heard the telephone crackle, Elsa asked for the manager and, when his deep voice echoed a little about the room, she said:

'M'sieu, the lady and gentleman who occupied this suite before us—can you give me their address, please?'

There was no pause from the other end, and I saw Elsa's fingers tighten about the telephone. The Jewess remained quite immobile. She had a statuesque beauty which even in her race must have been exceptional, although in a few years she would be fat and coarse. I swallowed at the constriction which threatened to come into my throat, for undoubtedly Elsa was receiving an answer she did not like.

'Yes, I will do that,' she said at last, and turned to the woman. Her disappointment must have been considerable but she hid it completely, and smiled in a friendly fashion.

'May I have your name, mam'selle?'

'It is Weiner—Mitzi Weiner.'

'Then I should call you fräulein,' said Elsa. 'Your parents were requested to move, and I believe they are at the *Hôtel Berliner*. They left that message for you.'

'Thank you so much,' said the other, and she stepped towards the door. I wished that I could rise in my chair and strike her.

'Fräulein,' I said in a harsh voice.

'Can I help you?' she asked, standing with a hand on the door.

'There is a matter for discussion,' I said. 'The interruption which was forced on us when we arrived here was unfortunate. I do not, I trust, need to tell you of the wisdom of discretion.'

She looked at me boldly.

'I remember nothing but that I entered a room rudely, and was received most courteously.'

'It is well to remember that,' I said. 'You may go.'

Lest there be those who wonder that my manner was so abrupt, it is wise to say that the attitude of all true Germans to Jews is one of scarcely veiled scorn. By then any man would have recognised her race, and even in unoccupied France it was known that a Jew had no right to respect, and no laws to protect them.

'Thank you,' she said. 'And you, Fräulien.' She bowed a little, and went out.

Almost before the door had closed on her, Elsa moved in the wake of Joachim, towards the ante-room. She was to follow the fine Fräulein Weiner, and make sure not only that she went to *l'Hôtel Berliner*, but that she saw von Stroem; despite the word from the manager I did not doubt that the talk of 'parents' was a lie. The manager was, of course, a Frenchman.

I was left alone.

It is not good to be alone in a strange hotel when one cannot move. I could, of course, have wheeled my chair and summoned the staff, but I wanted only coffee, and none in France would be worth drinking; I had not yet had time to hand a ration of my coffee to the manager for serving when I called for it. But there was some in the Thermos, in a small case which Joachim had carried in. I wheeled my chair towards it, but the case had been put down in a position where I could not reach it without straining my side too much.

How I wanted that coffee!

It has become to me something like whisky becomes to a drunkard; it is impossible to do without.

My stick was resting in the chair at my side. I took it and moved my good left leg to the floor. For one moment as I made the effort the veins stood out on my forehead and neck, and I felt the blood rushing through my head. But I reached my feet, and stood swaying for a moment, quite dizzy.

That passed.

My stick is hooked at the top; I slid it along my hand and put the hook into the handle of the small case, then drew it towards me. That simple action gave me more confidence—I was not so weak as I imagined. I poured the coffee into the cup-cap, and the warm beverage coursed through my veins. Soon I felt a new man. I thumped my stick on the carpeted floor—*thump*—a pause—*thump*. I enjoy doing that; I know that the sound of my approach strikes fear into the minds of those who have something to hide. It is an art, that *thump*—a pause—*thump*. I need not, of course, hit the floor so heavily, but the art has been developed to a high pitch.

That too helped to put me in a better humour.

A special long-chair on wheels—there are any number in Paris, for I have spent a long time in the French capital, and one had been brought to Vichy at my orders, through Brunning—was there and I sat in it. I placed myself near the telephone, for it was possible that Brunning, Joachim or Elsa would call me. Then I concentrated on the events which I have so far recorded.

I did not give much attention to Fräulein Weiner.

Elsa would discover all that there was to find out. I was far more concerned with Fuller and Joachim—would Joachim be able to follow the Englishman?

Why had Fuller been waiting for me, I wondered.

There was, also, the anxiety which could not be kept any longer at bay—anxiety at the fact that he had not only discovered that I would be in Vichy—*ach*, he had followed me, his talk of the battle over Munich had shown that—but that he had known at what hotel I would be, and what room at the hotel.

I suddenly tightened my hands. What right had he in the hotel? How could he be there, even in the foyer, without attracting attention? By one way only—he must have booked a room, either earlier in the day or immediately after he had seen where I was going.

I lifted the telephone as that thought occurred to me.

'The manager,' I said, and immediately a smooth French voice answered me, speaking in German. I did not know the manager's name, but I already had reason to doubt his loyalty to the New Order, and I took pleasure in rasping:

'You can speak in French—I understand quite well.'

'*Mais oui, m'sieu,*' he said, and then—a thousand curses on him!—he began to talk so swiftly in French that I could

catch only a word here and there. Nor was it possible for
me to interrupt him for several seconds, for I was endeavouring to understand what he said. But finally I lost my
patience, and roared:

'Silence! You speak too indistinctly, speak more plainly.'

'Mais oui, m'sieu,' said that swine of a manager, and he
spoke very slowly and in child-French, as if to a man whose
acquaintance with the language was gathered only from
text-books. 'I was expressing the hope that there is nothing
more m'sieu requires. That his stay in Vichy will be a happy
one. That it will be the first of many. We are honoured to
have so distinguished a visitor . . .'

'You are insolent!' I barked.

'M'sieu!' How cleverly the beast put reproach into his
voice; it was almost as if I had done him an injustice.

'I wish to know who has booked rooms here today,' I
said. 'In particular, a man . . .' I described Fuller carefully,
and it was necessary to repeat the description three times,
until finally he said in a tone which sounded convincing:

'There is no such man registered here, m'sieu.'

'How can you be sure?' I demanded. 'Do you see every
man who registers here?'

'Yes, m'sieu,' said the manager suavely. 'That was suggested by the German Consul. It makes sure that none
whom I do not personally inspect can take a room. Thus
the possibility of suspected persons hiding here is eliminated. The country, alas, is full of spies, and those disloyal
to the Government of France and the aged Marshal.'

'There was such a man in the foyer just before I entered,'
I said.

'I was there myself, I am sure—but m'sieu! I recall!'
Positively he sounded excited, pretending it pleased him to
help me. What a hypocrite the man was! 'There was such
a man! I inquired his business. He told me that he was
from the Press, and that he wished to interview Baron von
Horssell on his arrival. I dealt with him as he deserved—
I told him that Herr Horst was arriving, that I knew of no
Baron von Horssell in Vichy, although there was such a
man who was venerated in all the countries controlled by
the Third Reich. He went off, believe me, m'sieu, with the
flea in his ear. I would not allow him to set eyes on you.'

'It is well,' I grunted, while my stomach revolted at such nauseating lies.

I rang off, but hardly had I done so than the telephone rang. I lifted it quickly, to hear Elsa saying:

'I have been waiting for some minutes. Advise Herr Horst immediately that I am waiting.'

'I speak, Elsa,' I said. 'The fools did not advise me. What have you to say?'

I sensed from her voice that she was excited, and from that I deduced that her news was good.

'I was able to follow her to *l'Hôtel Berliner*,' she said. 'There is a family named Weiner staying, but I believe that is a trick. She went to *his* apartment. And,' continued Elsa before I could comment, thus forcing me to give full attention when I wanted to digest that confirmation of the Jewess's association with von Stroem, 'there is another thing. There had been a shooting attempt at the Baron von Stroem outside the hotel. It was filled with gendarmes and also the Gestapo. Undoubtedly the attack was done well.'

'It is *very* good,' I said. 'Did they find who attempted the shooting of Herr Baron?'

'No,' said Elsa, with a lilt of pleasure in her throaty voice, 'the wretched assassin escaped. von Stroem refuses to see anyone, although he allowed the woman to enter.'

'And is there more?' I asked.

'No,' said Elsa, 'but it would perhaps be wise if I stayed near for a while.'

'You may do so,' I said, and rang off. I stared at the telephone for some seconds, and then I seemed to hear her words again: '*the wretched assassin escaped*'.

I began to laugh. Brunning had performed excellently. It was perfect, perfect! I would even tolerate some degree of friendship between him and Elsa! He deserved some reward. I laughed until I had to hold my sides. It was painful, but still I laughed. Soon von Stroem would need help, and he would get it—help from the man who had fired at him!

How I laughed!

I made so much noise that I did not hear the door open behind me, the door of the ante-room. Not until the new-comer was within a yard of me did I become aware of his

presence, when between gusts of laughter he said:
'Are you so amused, Baron?'

It was as if the laughter and all things concerned with
it had been cut out of me with a keen knife, and I felt the
actual pain in my stomach. I heard the voice and recognised it and yet I did not believe it—I could not believe it.

'Let me turn your chair for you,' said the voice. A hand
was placed on the back of my chair, and it was swung round
so swiftly that I was forced to lean heavily on my right
side. For that alone I would have struck the man, had I
been able.

But I was not.

I was alone, and in my chair—and I was turned about
as a child might be turned, to stare into the eyes of Bruce
Murdoch, to see his fresh face and fair hair, to see the
derisive smile on his lips, to know that the man I hated
above all others had me at his mercy.

13

Bruce Murdoch

The photograph which I had shown von Stroem had not
lied in any single detail. I think I saw that hated face magni-
fied threefold. It was perhaps six feet away from me, but
I did not see his shoulders or his figure—I saw only his
face. Even the tiny mole on the cleft of his chin was clearly
visible.

When he had spoken I had received the shock; I was over
it quickly, and composed my features. My teeth were clenched, and the slight movement of my lower jaw seemed
to move my whole head, and there was even a noise in my
ears from it.

'You should be more careful, Murdoch,' I said. 'I dislike
being moved abruptly.'

'Not bad,' said Bruce Murdoch in the faintly derisive
manner which only he possesses. Fuller talks nonsense—

similar nonsense to Murdoch—but does not present it half as effectively as this man who, I knew, was of Scottish parents but had been bred in England.

'Not bad at all,' repeated Murdoch. 'If you go on like that you'll get quite polished in riposte, won't you?' He sat on the arm of a chair, a favourite position of his. He had shown no gun; perhaps he knew that I did not make a habit of carrying one with me. 'Have you had a busy night?' he inquired.

'I shall have busier,' I growled.

'I hope not,' said Murdoch, and he spoke almost as if he meant it. 'You know, Baron, you're too old for this kind of thing. Old and infirm—no offence meant.'

He did mean offence, of course; he hated me as much as I hated him, although he did not show it so plainly, and always covered it with smooth words. He knew that the thing which would anger me most was reference to my infirmity, and he would never stop making references when it suited him.

'You will change your opinion,' I said.

'Well,' said Murdoch, sliding one hand from his pocket and bringing with him a small cigarette case, 'that's a matter of opinion. Do you mind if I smoke?' He contrived to take out a cigarette and light it one-handed. I inferred from that that in his left hand there was an automatic. He blew smoke above my head, and gave the impression of being a fully contented and satisfied man. It was unbelievable that this was Vichy, that an Englishman could behave as he was doing here.

'Thanks,' he said. 'Well, von Horssell, let's get to business. Mick Fuller's had a chat with you. He could have killed you, you know—and killed the lovely Elsa. Isn't she putting on a little weight,'

Did the fool not know that Joachim might return at any moment, and that Brunning might also arrive? Of course he did not! He had seen the others go out, and he believed that he was safe. But not for long—*I* knew that. I was not, therefore, perturbed; there would be an interruption from Joachim or Brunning.

'I could also kill you now,' he said.

I showed my teeth in a smile.

86

'Proceed,' I said.

He laughed; he admires courage, as do I.

'So you're still full of guts,' he remarked. 'In a way that's a pity, Baron. I hoped that I'd convinced you that there is nothing you can usefully do. There isn't, you know. von Stroem did you a grave disservice when he dragged you out of your retirement.'

'He gave me an opportunity for serving my country,' I rasped.

'Oh, he would dress it up all right,' said Murdoch. 'But you're not noticing things as you used to.'

His accursed air of superiority is infuriating. Yet I knew this man to be one of the cleverest in the service of the British Intelligence. I knew that there had been a time when he had deceived me—yes, me!—into believing that he had changed sides, and that he would work for the New Order in England. I applied every test that it was possible to apply; I thought I had coerced him from Mary Dell, from Sir Robert Holt—whom he disrespectfully called the Pink 'Un, I am told—and from his friends. But he deceived me, and had been able to turn defeat into temporary victory for himself.*

And he had said I was not noticing things, the fool! Nothing that had happened had escaped me.

'What von Stroem didn't tell you,' said Murdoch gently, 'is his full knowledge of the situation in France. You haven't been here long enough to notice it. The lies of Dakar and Marseilles are exploded myths by now. France is seething. Nine Frenchmen in ten would take up arms if they could, and against your precious Fatherland, Baron. Not a nice thought, nearly a year after you have over-run the country, is it?'

'It is a lie,' I said.

'von Stroem would say so,' admitted Murdoch, and he laughed. 'What a fool you are, Baron! Can you imagine for a moment that if von Stroem could get himself out of his difficulties without help he would not do so? Hadn't it occurred to you that he was at the end of his tether but would not admit it to Hitler?'

'No man explains failure to the Leader,' I said.

* *The Withered Man,* by Norman Deane.

'No, I suppose not. He who says "it can't be done is the worst specimen of Hun". Original but not spontaneous, I made it up while I was waiting for the others to go.'

'From where?' I demanded.

I did not mind how long this absurd conversation continued, for I knew that every minute which I gained increased the likelihood of the return of Joachim, or the arrival of Brunning.

I do not blame Murdoch for his effort to make me suspicious of von Stroem, and to sow the seed of discord between us. Little did he know how prepared I was!

'From where?' Murdoch repeated my question. 'What from where—oh, the ante-room, of course.'

I gripped the arm of my wheel chair.

'You were in there all the time?'

'From the moment of your arrival,' said Murdoch sardonically. 'First Joachim then Elsa dashed out in a great hurry after Fuller, while I hid behind the wardrobe. A serviceable piece of furniture. Of course Joachim might have turned round, and in that case I would have been compelled to shoot him. I wouldn't like that. I have quite an affection for Joachim.'

I barked: 'What!'

'Does it surprise you?' he asked, as if himself surprised. 'It should not. In the past few months I've studied your entourage using your own method of spying out the ground before walking on it. I don't like Elsa, but then we've met before. I don't like Brunning—he's a Nazi half-wit with a half-wit's cunning, a worthy protégé of yours, my dear Baron!'

He had a way of saying 'my dear Baron' which made me writhe; it was insolence to the last degree, for my title has been in my family for ten generations. But I did not allow myself to lose my temper, although by then a strange thought was growing in my mind.

I was playing for time—*and so was Murdoch*.

There could be no other explanation of his casual manner. He was in no hurry, but he must have taken into account the possibility that assistance would arrive for me. He would not take that risk without good reason: *why, then, was he waiting?*

88

I confess that it made me uneasy, but I did not show that. Nor did I make any reply to his estimate of Brunning's capability. It was well that he should deceive himself.

'And you didn't rise to that bait!' exclaimed Murdoch, making a foolish noise with his tongue against the roof of his mouth. 'Your iron self-control is much in evidence. Where were we—oh, yes, Joachim. Do you know, that man is a freak. He likes you for yourself.'

I said: 'Joachim and his family have served me since I was a child.'

Murdoch's expression changed.

For a moment I believed that he had heard the sound of an approach, and my heart leapt. But there was silence outside; that was not the explanation of his change of expression. He had realised some error he had made, then. Perhaps he saw for the first time that he was wasting time that for him would be invaluable.

At last he said: 'I don't believe it. You—a *child*?'

Then I lost my temper! I was goaded beyond myself. I had been gripping the handle of my stick, which was free from its rest, and I lifted it and struck at him. The movement took him by surprise, but he evaded the sweeping blow except that it scratched his cheek. I saw the blood welling and drew a fierce satisfaction. I would teach the fool to make that kind of joke with me!

Then he moved.

I do not know whether my own infirmity and inability to move swiftly increased my estimate of the speed of others, although I am often startled by a swift movement. But I can say with honesty that I have never known a man move as swiftly and effectively as Murdoch.

He came forward.

I thought he was going to strike me, although nothing in the past has suggested that he would strike a man as helpless as I except in emergency. Instead he clenched my left wrist, which as I have said is powerful; one would think it had strength which should be in my right also. But his pressure was so great, and so well-applied, that my fingers were nerveless. The stick dropped.

He picked it up and stood back. He was pale, and much of the brown tan which he had possessed when first I had met him had faded. He gave me the impression of being a man whose face had been bleached by constant darkness —as a man might look who has been in the solitary cell at Dachau for some weeks. Of course, there was no sign of wastage of flesh about him or his face; except for the whiteness he appeared to be in full health.

The red blood from the scratch made that pallor more obvious—and, in fact, enabled me to notice it for the first time.

He said in a low voice which indicates that he has been stirred out of his composure:

'Another mistake by von Horssell—you pile them up. However, I shall accept the premise that you were once a child. I wouldn't like the moral responsibility of your parents! It's as bad as fathering Stickelgruber.'

I said: '*What*?'

'Didn't you know that your pet's real name was Stickelgruber?' demanded Murdoch, in apparent surprise. 'His parents were born that way, and so was he. The Austrian half-wit, Stickelgruber; the Nazi leader, Adolf Hitler. You see, they rhyme.'

'Murdoch,' I said, although the words would hardly come from my lips for my throat was constricted and I had difficulty in breathing, 'for that insult I will kill you with my own hands.'

'Hand,' said Murdoch sharply.

'*Hands*,' I said, emphasising the plural. 'I will do that myself—no other shall have the opportunity. But first I shall . . .'

'Spare us the sadistic touch,' said Murdoch. 'Where were we?'

I did not interrupt: I wanted to re-establish myself after that insult to the greatest man Germany has ever seen, the man who will mould a new world.

'Oh, yes, Joachim,' Murdoch said. 'Do you know, dear Baron, he is the one who really puts you first. All your servants, all those who fawn before you, those who eat with you and rob you right and left—Brunning, Elsa, Lieber, the rest of the bunch—all they want is your money and your protection.'

I glared at him; I could not speak.

90

'Even Elsa,' he added softly. 'You have a peculiar combination of parental, avuncular and marital right in her, haven't you? Or you think you have. Have you never noticed that whenever she goes off for a day it is always when Brunning is away on business? But no,' added Murdoch quickly, as if he wished he had not said that. 'I won't play gooseberry—let them have their pleasures. You may even have given them your blessing.'

Then he stopped, while I thought of Elsa and Brunning, and the evidence I had seen—I could not deny the probable truth of Murdoch's words. For the first time his mockery and derision affected me. I began to feel fear of those I trusted.

14

Brunning Reports

I doubt whether I would have paid any attention to Murdoch's innuendo but for what I had already suspected, and then I realised the real object of his visit. He wished to make me distrustful of everyone. Of von Stroem, of Elsa, of Brunning. He wanted me to feel as if I were entirely alone, knowing as he did that I could not work without others.

I think he realised that I understood. My breathing, which had started to choke me again, cleared. I looked across the room at the table where I had left the Thermos flask of coffee. When he had turned my chair he had made it impossible for me to reach it.

I was surprised by his next action.

He stepped across the room, took the flask, poured out some coffee—the last of it I saw as I watched the steam rising from the cup-cap—and handed it to me. He did not take the opportunity thus presented to him of gloating over me: worse, I think that for a moment he was sorry for me, and there is nothing worse than pity from any man, while from Murdoch it was unbearable. Yet I wanted the drink.

I took the cup, and said: 'I am obliged.'

He watched me drinking, and must have seen the way in which it stimulated me, for he said:

'What is in that?'

'It is just coffee,' I said.

'Real coffee?' He widened his eyes. 'So there is some in Europe. Baron, I congratulate you. If it's possible to get a thing you certainly get it.'

I said: 'I have already reminded you that I shall get you.'

'You forget the operative words "if it's possible",' he said lightly, and he stubbed out his cigarette. 'I've talked a lot, haven't I?'

'Too much,' I said.

'Oh, I don't know,' said Murdoch. 'I've been waiting for this opportunity for a long time, Baron. I've been watching you, and I've seen you at your window very often. It was annoying not to be able to talk about the old days.'

He laughed at me.

He had good reason, for a fool would have guessed my reaction to learning that he had been close enough to my house to watch me in my study. Of course, he might have been lying, but I had proof that Angell and Fuller had been working in the grounds, and there was no reason to disbelieve him. All the time that I had been brooding over him, and dreaming thoughts of vengeance, *he* had been watching me.

Why, why, why?

I was not, of course, afraid of him, in that room or anywhere else. Again I was comforted by the knowledge that he did not propose to do me actual violence. The shooting at my house made that puzzling, but I dismissed the factor as unimportant. Angell and Fuller had shot at me without instructions; there could be no other explanation.

Murdoch took out another cigarette, but allowed his left hand to remain in his pocket about the gun I was sure was there. Even when he had poured out the coffee he had not moved that hand.

'Yes, I've watched you, and waited for this discussion— I've often wondered when it would be possible, Baron. Now I shall tell you the main purpose.'

I did not speak.

'You've come, of course, to try to find Mondel,' went on Murdoch. 'Oddly, the Führer'—how he sneered that word!—'wants to see him. The interview is only to be half-faked. Perhaps you haven't realised the power which Mondel has been acquiring. Like many other Germans you have been trying to ingratiate yourself with Petain, through Laval, and have seen in Mondel just the owner of many papers which only his foreign money can subsidise. You haven't realised how powerful he is getting. You did not know that he has won a great measure of support from the common people. You do,' he added very softly, 'make the one essential mistake in everything you attempt, von Horssell. It seems a German prerogative. You ignore the importance of the common man.'

'They are cattle,' I snapped.

'No,' said Murdoch softly, 'you *think* they are cattle. Despite your eight years of misrule, despite the way you have taught your children, despite your marching and your flag-waving and your cry for *lieberstrumm*, despite the poison you have put into their minds, *they are getting suspicious of you, von Horssell*. Even the youth, the wonderful Nazi youth. They know their leaders have continuously lied. They are learning that human beings are being treated in occupied countries like dirt. They are beginning to wonder what you really think of *them*.'

'They are of the chosen race,' I snapped.

'So were fifty or sixty thousand who were drowned when you started your ill-fated invasion,' flashed Murdoch. 'So are tens of thousands in the concentration camps. It is slowly filtering into their empty minds—minds *you* emptied —that the only chosen people are the thugs and pimps and prostitutes in Berchtesgarten and in the Wilhelmstrasse. Yes, my *dear* Baron, you have underestimated the importance of the masses, but your own fools aren't ripe for revolt yet. The French are. Mondel knows that. Mondel has insidiously ranged the masses behind him. Didn't von Stroem tell you that? Didn't von Stroem tell you that Mondel can sway thirty-five million people, and that they must be swayed your way if you are to hold France?'

I could not believe this.

Yet there was fear in my mind that there could be a measure of truth in it. von Stroem had been summoned to Berchtesgarten—none went there without such a summons, and few for approbation. He was worried about Mondel. He had told me a story which had appeared sufficient in itself, but I remembered that when I had first heard the story I had wondered whether there was more behind it. I had actually asked von Stroem why there should be such a fuss about an interview which could be printed whether it took place or not.

More: I had asked what it would matter if Mondel was killed by Murdoch, had even suggested it would be an advantage. von Stroem had disagreed. I saw now why; Mondel had a far greater power in France than von Stroem had dared to suggest. Mondel's disappearance was causing real anxiety in the minds of the Party leaders. Such concern could only be caused by the disappearance of a man who really mattered.

I *did* believe Murdoch.

He was watching me with those veiled grey eyes of his, no longer sardonic or amused or mocking but as if he was making a big effort to read my thoughts. I stirred in my chair, to ease a little pressure from my right thigh, and I said smoothly:

'All of this is interesting, Murdoch. I am always interested in what fantasies the English are to indulge next. So you would have me believe that a fool of a Frenchman matters! Ho-ho-ho!' I laughed. 'That is a fine joke! But proceed, my *dear* Murdoch. You were to be good enough to tell me the chief object of your visit. I should dislike to rob you of the final sentence of your joke.'

He regarded me with an expression which I had seen before—a puzzling one, which I can never quite understand.

'And you would like to hear the end, wouldn't you? About Mondel. I had one particular task—the Pink 'Un gave me it. He also asked me to send you his regards,' added Murdoch mockingly, and I could believe that fool of a pink-and-white man, Holt, would do such a thing. They are all mad, the British—that is often said as a joke, and too few people take it seriously enough. In their madness is their strength, that peculiar ability to do the thing which no sane man would even attempt.

'The end,' I said, laughing again but more silently. 'I am longing to hear it, Murdoch.'

'Hold your breath,' said Murdoch, and he straightened up from the chair. 'I am going to take Mondel to England, Baron. How do you like the idea?'

.   .   .   .   .

I am not easily impressed.

Moreover, I had acted with considerable cunning, and knew that I had contrived to deceive Murdoch into thinking that I was much less concerned than I was. I had not known what to expect. I had believed it possible he would say that he had come to kill Mondel, and that would have been understandable. But to take him to England—no, it was impossible!

He laughed at me.

'Quite a shock, wasn't it, Baron? Look at every angle thoroughly, won't you. At the moment if Mondel died it would be awkward, but you could overcome it. There might be riots but you could quell them—you're very good with the truncheon. And with the machine-gun, although you mustn't waste ammunition, it's hard to come by these days. But if Mondel doesn't bow to Adolf's orders, off goes his head, and you'll suppress his newspapers. But once he's in England—a supporter of Free France—that will be a different kettle of fish, Baron! Suppress all the papers you like, but you can't supress the radio. They listen —they listen in Berlin and in Berchtesgarten, so believe me they listen in France. Mondel, silenced by Hitler, driven out of the country, a supporter of de Gaulle.'

I said with an effort: 'You will never succeed.'

'Oh, but I will,' said Murdoch. 'I'm halfway to it already. And . . .' He stopped for a moment, and the mockery went out of his eyes. I was almost convinced that he was sincere. 'Listen to me, Baron. I sent you into retirement. I defeated you in England. At the time I would gladly have killed you, but I knew one thing—you were sincere in your loyalties, you did a wonderful job, a misguided one perhaps but something I had to admire. After this failure you won't be retired, you will be hanged. Or shot. They won't let you live. von Stroem is anxious you should be the victim, not he—he knows I can do it. So turn down the offer, Baron. You are a sick man, they can't blame you.'

I stared at him through mists that fogged my mind.

If I failed, it might well be as he said. But there was a thing he could not understand, and would never understand. *If* I failed I deserved to die. I would not wish to live. I have one purpose—to serve my Fatherland. If I failed in so immense an undertaking, whatever happened to me was unimportant.

I said: 'I shall not fail, Murdoch. Any man who failed would not be worthy of living.'

He regarded me oddly. There was silence for some seconds. Then he said in a detached voice:

'You really mean that, don't you?'

'I mean it all,' I assured him. 'You will not win, Murdoch. I shall present Mondel to the Leader at the appointed time.'

He frowned and stared for some seconds, then shrugged, laughed, and moved towards the door. I found it hard to believe that he was going to leave as abruptly as Fuller had done, but that appeared to be in his mind.

'All right,' he said, 'if you won't play ball you can play hunt-the-hangman. An interesting pastime. Did you know that the meeting with your Führer is for Friday, at two in the afternoon? It is now Wednesday morning—a little after five o'clock and nearly daylight.'

He *knew* the time of the appointment, which was more than I did. He could not have chosen a more disconcerting note on which to leave me, but while I was grappling with the further evidence of his accursed knowledge there was an interruption.

I did not hear the approach of footsteps; I am sure that Murdoch did not. The first I heard was the opening of the door, which squeaked a little. I cursed the squeak, for it gave Murdoch a moment of warning. He moved to the ante-room door—it was the main door which was opening —and he drew his left hand from his pocket. He *was* carrying a gun.

He fired at the door.

The bullet went over my head. I did not duck, for it was useless to do so—if he wished to shoot me he could no matter what I tried to do to avoid it. I heard a bullet splinter into the wood of the door, and the faint hiss of the shot as it was fired—there was an efficient silencer on Murdoch's gun.

I saw Brunning!

He was framed for a moment in the doorway, and I saw the stab of flame which came from his revolver. This time there was a roar which echoed through the room. It would raise an alarm and bring so many people that Murdoch could not possibly escape.

He fired again.

I saw a spot of red on Brunning's hand as he pulled the door to protect himself. He should have thought of me but in the excitement it was easy to understand that his first consideration was to prevent Murdoch's escape.

Again Murdoch approached the ante-room door.

He reached it, turned the handle, then he pulled. But the door this time did not open; it had been locked!

Brunning must have done that.

How I wished that I had a revolver then; I could have reduced my personal risk to an absolute minimum. But it did not appear as if Murdoch wished to kill me—that was a thing which I could not understand for a long time.

He backed to the window.

But as he did so there was a noise from outside. Not the excited cries of people who had been disturbed; the silence for the first few minutes after the loud shot had been ominous, and it occurred to me that in France they were learning the wisdom of discretion—a shot often meant the death of a traitor, and interference as often the death of a curious man.

No, heavy footsteps sounded.

I heard a word of command, and then the main door and the ante-room were opened simultaneously as Murdoch reached the window and flung it up. Men poured into the room, men in the uniform of storm-troopers! I could not count them, and I did not try. I knew Murdoch could not escape.

15

Elsa Reports

Murdoch had one leg over the window sill.

That remarkable faculty of his for moving with a speed which appears unbelievable had never been demonstrated so vividly. I strained forward in my chair, my breath coming heavily through my open lips. My eyes were glowing, for I knew the man must come back or else be killed.

He did not come back.

He flung his other leg over the sill, and as he did so Brunning—who had entered with the men from the passage door—gave the order to fire.

A volley of shots rang out. Bullets smashed through the window above Murdoch's head, and one was so badly aimed that it hit the wall. Murdoch disappeared. I saw his head and shoulders fall downwards, much as a film will move when the operator handles his projector badly. I saw a smile—yes, a smile of derision!—on his face before he went from my sight.

Brunning was cursing the men.

Their shooting was abominable, but I could not believe that Murdoch had escaped unhurt. I *would* not believe it. At least eight bullets had been fired at him, one at least must have taken effect. But there had been no suggestion of pain on his face as he had dropped from sight, and no sign of blood.

For once I regretted the fact that I always have a suite on the ground or first floor, so that there is not too much difficulty with my chair. I tried to remember what the courtyard was like outside the hotel. I could not. I saw Brunning, whose wound could be no more than a scratch, push the storm troopers out of his way, and reach the window.

As he looked out there was a report of a shot from outside, and a bullet came in at the window. Plaster sprayed from the ceiling. Brunning pulled his head back sharply, and snarled to the men:

'Two of you follow him! The others, round to the tradesmen's entrance!'

He was already on the way to the door. There was a moment of hesitation amongst the men—Brunning should have been more precise, should have named the two to go through the window.

I rasped: 'You—and you!'

I indicated the men with my hand, but one drew back although the other went forward promptly enough, and began to climb through.

The first said: 'Excellency, we are plain marks for the bullets...'

'You will be a plainer mark in front of a brick wall!' I snarled, and he obeyed me.

There was another shot.

It caught the craven in the face, and he shrieked. He turned about, his hands to his eyes, and I could see that the bullet had gone through his mouth. There was just a moment while he continued to shriek and then he fell down, writhing in front of me.

I heard no more shooting, although I could hear footsteps resounding as if men were running on metal. I wheeled my chair towards the window. One wheel went over the outstretched leg of the wounded man, and wrenched my side severely. I pressed on. Doing so, I passed my stick which Murdoch had rested against the wall. When I was as near the window as I could get I eased myself forward, leaning on my stick and my sound leg. In that half-standing position I was able to see outside.

Dawn was coming.

I had not realised it because of the blackout, but it was stealing across the sky, grey and vague and yet light enough to let me see what was below. The hotel was built like a triangle, and the space in the centre was covered with iron roofing—the roof, I remembered then, of the main lounge on the ground floor. At one end—or more accurately one corner—of the triangle there was an arched doorway. The storm-trooper who had not hesitated was already going through it.

There was no sign of Murdoch.

The length of his fall had been negligible. By stretching

99

himself to his full length and swinging on his hands, his feet would have nearly touched the iron. But he could have reached the doorway at such speed only if he had been unhurt.

I crouched and stared for some minutes. My rage was frightening even to me, for when I lose my self-control my neck tightens, I feel as if I am choking. Even the cold air from outside did nothing to ease me. I had to struggle for each breath, and I was quite unaware of a step behind me, or of a firm hand on my shoulder.

'You must rest, Ludvic.'

It was Elsa. In her voice there was a soft and caressing note and one which I have learned to relish. It soothes me in my bad moments more than anything else I know. I allowed myself to sink back in my chair, and she turned me away from the window and wheeled me into the bedroom next door. We frequently share a room; it comforts me at nights, when my hatred of Murdoch turns my sleep to a succession of nightmares. Sometimes in the past months she has read to me while I have rested, sweating from every pore, and her quiet voice has done much to help.

I was aware of a strange thing.

I did not want her to go. I was afraid that she would never come back. I was weak, of course, and my mind had had too much to grapple with for the past twelve hours. The suspicions of her and Brunning were vivid in my mind; I wanted to disbelieve it.

I remember seizing her forearm with my left hand.

I remember that for a brief instant Murdoch was forgotten, with all that his escape might mean.

'Elsa,' I said, as well as I could speak the words; my voice is at times incoherent but she had learned to understand me. 'Elsa, tell me it is all untrue, it must be untrue.'

'What is it, Ludvic?' she asked quietly.

'You—and Brunning. There is nothing between you, there must not be. You are mine, Elsa, I cannot do without you. I did not realise until now how much I depend on you, how much I need you.' I increased my grip until it must have hurt her badly, but I did not do it to pain her, and I believe she knew that. She made no effort to release her arm but said in the same gentle voice:

100

'Who has been lying to you, Ludvic? Brunning is a good servant, that is all. At times he is innocent and impertinent, but I can control him. Why, for a friend I would rather be with Joachim!'

'Joachim?' I croaked. 'He—he is too old. He is too faithful to betray me. Brunning would, I know he would! Elsa, you will always be faithful to me, you will think of no other man.'

'What men I know,' she said very quietly, 'are essential to our cause, Ludvic, you know that.'

'And Murdoch—Murdoch lied about Brunning?'

She stepped back a pace.

She could not go far because I had her arm, but I saw the expression in her eyes—one that might have been of horror or of fear, but mostly of consternation.

'*Murdoch!*' she whispered. 'He—he has been here?'

'Never mind that!' I tried to shout, but the words were no more than mouthings. 'He told me you and Brunning consorted, he said . . .'

She had regained her composure; it must have been a shock beyond thinking when she had heard of Murdoch's visit. With her free hand she smoothed my face; it was strangely comforting. Then she drew a handkerchief from the pocket of her long coat, and began to wipe the perspiration from my forehead and my cheeks. She is very beautiful, and so gentle. I put my face against her breast.

'He was lying,' she said. 'I have no time for Brunning. I swear that, Ludvic.'

'It is enough,' I said. 'I am glad, Elsa.'

'And now,' she said, 'you must rest. No!' Her voice sharpened when I tried to look towards the door. 'You *must* rest. There is time for everything later. I will watch for Murdoch and the others. Perhaps,' she added—I think solely to reassure me, 'he has not escaped. I met Brunning and many others hurrying.'

She had freed her arm, and then from her handbag—resting on a table—she took a hypodermic syringe. It was not filled with the serum—only I allow that to be injected—but with an opiate that would make me sleep. I wanted sleep. My mind was beginning to go through all Murdoch had said, and I could not cope.

101

She unfastened the special flap in the thigh of my trousers and I felt the single prick of the needle—she did not falter, as Fritz had done earlier.

'I will get you to bed as Joachim is not here,' she said. 'Can you move—just a little?' I made myself, and then stretched out on the bed, the opiate going through my body like a soothing oil on a burn. My mind grew empty. I was in the coma which precedes sleep. I felt her taking off my coat, my boots, my collar and tie. She was strong and yet gentle. I loved her hands about me.

I slept.

I do not know how long I was asleep but I can remember vividly that when I awakened I was so refreshed that it was difficult for me to believe that I had been in the frame of mind which had made me talk as I had to Elsa. That in fact was the first thought in my mind, and I regretted my weakness. I sensed the difference in myself when I sat up. That is normally a difficult thing, and I often call for Joachim's assistance when I am in a strange room; my own room is fitted with handles in the wall and on the bed, so that wherever I am I can pull myself to my feet, or to a sitting position.

I was able to think over what had happened without the clogging mist which had harassed me so much on the previous day. I felt as I had often done in the past, when I knew that nothing was beyond my grasp, and to myself I laughed at the thought of Murdoch outwitting me. He would never take Mondel to England—nor would *he* ever return there! The accursed man had been lucky, he was always lucky. But I laughed at him.

Perhaps there is a psychological explanation of my mental *volte-face*. For the first time for a long period I awakened to face a problem. I awakened with Murdoch near me, almost certainly in Vichy, a man of flesh and blood with whom I could grapple, not a distorted figure of imagery in my mind, out of reach and unlikely to be seen again.

I pressed the bell within reach.

Joachim entered almost as soon as my finger left the button; he had of course been waiting outside my door. He was smiling in his grave fashion, and what Murdoch had said about him made me see him in a new light. He was the one man in whom I could place reliance, a man in whom the tie of affection was deeper than that of gain. In some measure that was true; Joachim is paid enough, but not too much. He is a bachelor. He is at my call day and night.

'Good morning, Excellency,' he said. 'You have slept well?'

'Never better!' I replied, not hesitating to show him my return of spirits and strength. 'And you, Joachim—how does the French air agree with you, eh? And the French-women, eh?' I shook with laughter, and it was pleasant to see the smile on Joachim's face. 'Perhaps, Joachim, when we have finished with Murdoch you will take a short holiday. If you wish it, while we are in France. Yes?'

'My life is in your service, Excellency,' he said, but I could see that he was pleased and grateful for my thought.

'The Fräulein can care for me for a few days,' I said. 'In the past when business has taken you away she has done so, if not so well as you, Joachim. We will return to that subject later. I want coffee, and then I will be bathed. Is the Fräulein here,'

'She slept in the next room, Excellency, so as not to disturb you. She is still sleeping in the chair.'

'Inform her that when I am bathed I shall need to talk with her. Inform Brunning, also, that he will be needed at any time. Where is he?'

'In his room, Excellency.'

I did not think that there was much good news to report, and therefore I did not ask questions. It is not the truth to say that bad news travels faster than good; bad news, I find, reaches me slowly, and in circuitous routes—men do not care to admit failure to me.

When Joachim brought coffee, I heard Elsa's voice. Soon afterwards I took my shower, and Joachim rubbed me down. I urged him to rub more briskly. It was good to feel the sting of cold water, the chafing of a harsh towel. It was good to be alive!

von Stroem—poof! He would be out of favour and lucky to escape death. I had all the information I needed about

him. And he would try to trick me, Ludvic von Horssell
how I felt like laughing!

I had toast and more coffee for my breakfast before
permitting Joachim to relate his story. Until then I had
wanted my mind free from all additional details, so that I
could get the events of the previous afternoon and night
clear in my mind. They were there, and I would forget
nothing, not the slightest detail. I knew that this fit of comparative vigour would last for four or five days at the least,
perhaps for two or three weeks. I have known them before,
often when my mind has been stimulated by a problem
which no other man would dare to attempt to overcome.

Joachim was direct, as always, and detailed.

He had reached the foyer and had contrived to follow
Fuller, who had walked. The chase had lasted for nearly
an hour before Fuller had gone into a tenement house.
Joachim had obtained all details of the house, which was
even then being guarded by Gestapo men.

'At who's orders?' I asked.

'The Fräulein's, Excellency.'

'That is good. I will now see the Fräulein.'

There are women who would try to take advantage of
my weakness the night before—just as women will try to
find advantage from a drunken man. I knew that the Elsa
who had worked with me for so long would not. But I was
not sure whether she had changed. Naturally she would
have denied any liaison with Brunning the night before; the
denial did not mean that I must relax my watch on them.

She came in with her easy grace. She was dressed in a
severe tailor-made costume, with a white blouse that was
frilly at the breast, and folded to a deep V—which she
knows I like. She may have slept on a chair, but she
appeared to be quite rested and her eyes were clear and
bright.

'Good morning, Excellency!'

That relieved me; she was precise and formal in her manner, as she should be.

'Good morning,' I said, and I launched into questions
immediately. I wanted to know what had been done,
and was not surprised to learn that Brunning had failed
to find Murdoch. He did not know how the man had

104

escaped, but in the half-light it had been impossible to follow him far. I nodded acceptance, and asked for his personal report of the 'attack' on von Stroem.

Brunning came in, clicked his heels, bowed, and immediately plunged into a recital. It seemed as if my own good spirits and clearer mind were contagious; the others had it. His story was satisfactory. He had reached the hotel before von Stroem, and fired two shots, careful to miss him. Then he had escaped, without difficulty, but for safety's sake had not immediately come to me. When he had returned he had gone into the ante-room lest he should interrupt me with Elsa. He had heard voices, and listened. Then he had locked the ante-room door, and hurried for help. I had arranged for men of the storm-troop to be at hand, and he used them.

'You did well, Brunning,' I said when he had finished. 'Those dolts of men, they are to blame for his escape. There was a wounded man—did he die?'

'Yes, Excellency.'

'Have the carpet changed,' I said. 'It was soiled.'

'It has been done,' interpolated Elsa.

'Good! Now, Brunning, I hope that before night His Excellency von Stroem will have appealed for a personal assistant, and I shall strongly recommend you.'

I was interrupted by the ringing of the telephone, and picked it up at once. I had a premonition that it was von Stroem, and that was the case. I did not wish to make it seem that I knew of his mishap, and my voice was jovial.

'Good morning, Excellency! I have been waiting to hear from you. You enjoyed your first night in France, I trust?'

He was the reverse of jovial: his voice was thick, and I rejoiced in the knowledge of the bleakness of his thoughts. He would never have the satisfaction of gloating over me again; I could trap him whenever it suited me to do so.

'My night was disturbed,' he said. 'Before I reached my hotel I was shot at ...'

I exclaimed: 'Baron! You were *shot* at?'

'That is what I said,' snarled von Stroem. 'Some accursed assassin. Had the bullet been an inch closer it would have killed me, as it was I needed three stitches in my cheek and it needs constant attention. But that is not all, von

Horssell,' he went on, and I knew he had something to complain about. I did not think of it. I did not hear him. I looked at Brunning, and I think the man realised something of what had happened, for his face blanched.

I formed words, but did not utter them.

Brunning licked his lips, and even stood back a pace, while I thought of the terrible nearness of disaster which he had brought to me. von Stroem nearly a victim of a plan which, for me, could not operate successfully unless he remained alive for some days to come.

Brunning had nearly killed him.

Thus I did not hear at first what other thing von Stroem said. But I heard it the second time, for he shouted loud enough for the whole city to hear.

16

I am Cunning

It was with difficulty that I restrained myself from replacing the receiver before von Stroem had finished. I would have done but for the fact that the words I caught had importance, and there is no sense in allowing personal resentment to interfere with the progress of a matter in hand.

'Are you listening to me?' he bellowed. 'I tell you that I saw Fräulein Elsa at my hotel last night—why was that? Why should she come to me?'

First Brunning had failed, then Elsa.

I hesitated, still considering replacing the receiver, and then I decided that a protest in words would be more effective.

'Herr Baron,' I said harshly, 'you appear to imagine you are addressing a company of recruits. You forget yourself. When you are good enough to lower your voice I may perhaps hear and understand you.'

In the pause which followed I could hear his heavy breathing, but he was wise enough to see that I had reason for taking offence. Not that I think that in itself would have made him alter his tone; beneath his suave exterior he possessed an unbearable insolence. Other things forced him to alter his manner. His narrow escape had shaken him. It might well be that Brunning's crass negligence would after all serve a purpose, although I was not likely to let Brunning realise that. And not only was von Stroem becoming worried because of what he doubtless considered to be an effort on Murdoch's part to assassinate him: he was beginning to see that in asking for my help he had brought upon himself difficulties it would not be easy to overcome.

He repeated what he had said word for word, and made no spoken apology.

'I tell you that I saw Fraulein Elsa at my hotel last night —why was that? Why should she come to me?'

I said smoothly: 'I am sure Herr Baron is mistaken. The Fräulein was all the evening in this hotel.'

'It is not so! I tell you that I saw her!'

'I will question her,' I said. 'She is out at the moment, but I am expecting her soon. I can see one possible explanation of her visit, Herr Baron.'

'And that is?'

'You will scarcely wish me to discuss possibilities when the facts can shortly be ascertained,' I said. That would keep him thinking and puzzling, as I intended. 'But I am perturbed by the accident to you. Are you not closely guarded?'

'You know quite well that I prefer to work on my own,' rasped von Stroem, although I could detect the note of uncertainty in his voice.

'I know that very well,' I said. 'Tell me, Herr Baron, can you recall the details of the accident in which you were involved when Lirchner was killed? I am wondering,' I added before he could interrupt, 'whether it could have been an attempt, as that of last night, to kill you. Murdoch would gladly see you dead.'

He did not immediately answer, and I went on:

'Have there been other incidents, Herr Baron?'

'It is possible—I cannot be sure,' he said in a low-pitched voice. 'Nor am I sure that Lirchner was killed instead of me.' There was much doubt in his tone, and I smiled with satisfaction. 'I have no man I can trust implicitly,' he added. 'Already my movements are watched more closely than I like to think.'

'That is so,' I said. 'I—Herr Baron!' I paused, then added: 'I have an idea which might prove of service. I have sent for a man to meet me here—a reliable man named Voss. I have the Fräulein, Brunning and my servant here, and am myself well cared for. I will gladly spare Voss for you.'

Again he hesitated, and then said slowly—as I expected that he would:

'I do not know Voss, Excellency, but the thought is appreciated.'

'I understand your hesitation,' I said. 'It is perhaps regrettable that I cannot make any other suggestion. But I will come to see you, Herr Baron.'

'I am not incapacitated,' he said irritably. 'But there has been much delay—it is nearly noon now. I shall be glad to see you. What of you, Excellency?'

'That report will keep,' I said. I chuckled deep in my throat, keeping the mouthpiece from its hook so that he would be able to hear a little of it, and then I replaced the instrument. He would be waiting anxiously for my arrival; I had arranged to take control of the great man of mystery very well indeed!

But I could not show my jubilation.

Brunning had made a grievous error, and Elsa also. She should not have allowed herself to be seen. She was regarding me coolly—I have never known her afraid of me, although that is in some measure due to the degree of familiarity which has been unavoidable.

Brunning had regained control of his facial muscles, but was clearly apprehensive. He was standing rigidly to attention, his head bent a little. He was making a considerable effort to meet my eyes. I stared at him unspeaking for some seconds, and then slowly I raised my stick. The steel ferrule at one end was sharp and rough, and I moved it slowly towards his cheek. He did not move, and Elsa kept quite still, although she was watching me closely.

I pushed the ferrule against his cheek, gently at first, and then I drew it downwards in a sharp movement, pressing hard all the time. He flinched, but did not move. Blood welled from the jagged tear in his flesh.

I said: 'You have now a wound in the same place as Herr Baron von Stroem, but his was inflicted by a careless fool, yours was inflicted intentionally. You do not encourage trust in you, Brunning.'

He made no attempt to stem the flow of blood.

'Your pardon, Excellency. I do not understand.'

'Your shot hit von Stroem!' I snarled at him. 'Lies and denials will only make it worse—perhaps you could see everything clearly in the darkness,' I sneered. 'Perhaps, on the other hand, you knew that you injured him but preferred not to report it. It is not a practice to encourage.'

His tongue licked his square lips for a moment, and after some hesitation he said:

'I believed that I fired wide, Excellency. Had I known otherwise I would have reported it. I abase myself.'

'You will do well to remember that we cannot afford mistakes,' I said sharply. 'Wait in the ante-room.'

He clicked his heels and bowed, and then went out. Not once while he was in the room did he touch the scar on his cheek, although as he reached the door I saw that blood was trickling down to his chin. As the door closed behind him I smiled grimly, for I admired his self-restraint.

I turned to Elsa.

'He will not make similar errors again,' I said.

'Which part of me do you wish to mutilate?' she demanded in a low-pitched voice, and for a moment I thought that she was being humorous. I stared at her, but there was no change in her expression. I began to laugh—laughter was very easy that morning.

'Ho-ho-ho!' I roared. 'That is a good one, Elsa, that is a good one! But you mistake the time of the day—it is noon, not midnight!' I continued to laugh for some seconds, although I knew that by so doing I was weakening my position—I could not easily be severe about her own error.

I sometimes think that I am specially protected against mistakes; I thought so then.

I stopped laughing, and composed my face.

'You are fortunate that I am in good humour,' I said. 'One way and another von Stroem is not pleased with life, and we shall have Brunning working with him before the day is out. But—you were seen at *l'Hôtel Berliner*. Why?' I made it sound as if I knew an explanation would be forthcoming.

'That is not surprising,' said Elsa. 'I intended that I should be.'

I stared at her in amazement.

'You *intended* so?'

'Had you been less fatigued last night I would have told you then,' she said, taking a cigarette from a box on a small table and lighting it. 'Ludvic, in this business it is necessary for me to act on my own initiative at times. It was impossible to make full inquiries about the woman without showing myself at the reception desk. There were S.S. men and others in the foyer, and my inquiries would doubtless have been reported. So I asked not for her, but for von Stroem. I was told that he would see no one. I was not pleased, and I created some disturbance. The manager was extremely apologetic,' she added with the slow smile which shows her tongue. 'He explained that it was a matter of extreme delicacy. *Ach*, it was easy,' added Elsa. 'Without letting him think that I was interested in Mitzi Weiner, I discovered she had gone to von Stroem, and also demanded that I saw the book so that I found out the Baron's room number. Then I saw Frau Weiner was staying at the hotel. I inquired because the name was Jewish. It was so, he said, and he was apologetic, he did not like Jews. But special instructions had been made that the Weiners, husband and wife, could stay; and who was he to question instructions?'

'And so von Stroem not only consorts with Jews but arranges for the parents of his mistress to stay in hotels and to defile them,' I remarked. 'Surely von Stroem will have much to explain!'

'I had not thought of that,' said Elsa.

'It occurred to me immediately,' I said. 'The manager had received special orders—not perhaps straight from von Stroem, but inspired by the man. And so you made it obvious that you were there. And what excuse would you have given had he decided to see you?'

She laughed, the little vixen! Her tongue showed, and

110

she leaned over me, so that I could smell the subtle perfume which she uses. The frills of her blouse brushed against my forehead, before she moved back a little.

'Ludvic, must I tell you that? After the Baron's amorous advances in the air last night, what was more reasonable than I should go to see him once you had dismissed me? I shall tell him that. It would perhaps be well if I went ahead of you, so that I could complain that he had reported to you. It will put him under an obligation to me.'

I laughed again—how I laughed! I gripped her shoulder, my fingers sinking into her warm flesh, and I drew her close to me so that our eyes were no more than a foot apart. She laughed also, her white teeth and her red tongue close to me, her body shaking.

I released her at last.

'Yes, go and complain,' I said. 'He will have Brunning working for him, and you enamoured of him, and myself well-disposed towards him. Could a man ask for greater friendship!' I laughed again, although by then my side was proving painful with so much unusual movement.

She did not ask why I had first recommended Voss—it was obvious to her that it was wise to let von Stroem think that I was reluctant to part with Brunning. She put on her coat and her hat, and left soon afterwards, leaving me fully satisfied with the way events had gone.

The only possible trouble would be from Murdoch.

If only that man had not escaped ...

But it was useless and not like me to wish for things which could not be, and I thrust it aside. The previous night Murdoch had made a considerable impression on my mind, but I knew that he had talked for the sake of talking. There might, of course, be some degree of truth in what he had said about von Stroem, but I would do everything that was necessary to make sure that, if there was any degree of failure, von Stroem would suffer, not I.

The talk of Mondel was different.

Murdoch had said nothing which suggested that he had Mondel or that he knew where to find him. He had said 'it is half-done', or words to that effect. Words, vain words.

I rang for Joachim and Brunning.

There was a wash-basin in the ante-room, and Brun-

111

ning had used the interval to wash and to dress his cheek.

I said: 'Brunning, here is a fact to remember. Murdoch has a wound just as yours, and on the same cheek—it will not be easy for him to cover it. In the search for him, remember that.'

'Yes, Excellency.'

'Good! Now, I wish you to go to Schlesser, who as you know took over my organisation in Paris. Go by air. Bring back with you as swiftly as possible a complete record of the situation in Paris and in the rest of France. Not the official record,' I added contemptuously, 'not that which is dressed-up and prepared for consumption at Berchtesgarten—I want the truth. Make Schlesser understand that.'

'I will, Excellency.'

'Be back here as soon as you can, but if you are delayed, telephone me here. By delay, I mean if you will not be able to return by seven o'clock tonight. You understand?'

'I will not lose time,' promised Brunning.

'Take three men with you, and have an escort 'plane also—there is no purpose in taking chances, and we must disperse Murdoch's men quickly. Endeavour also to obtain information about Mondel, the French newspaper owner.'

'I will, Excellency.'

I nodded dismissal, and he went out.

Elsa had perhaps ten minutes start of me, and I thought that ample time for her purpose. I told Joachim to wheel me out, and five minutes later I was on my way to *l'Hôtel Berliner*. It was not far, and I did not go by car. Joachim pushed my wheel chair on the pavement, and many people stepped aside, even apologised for getting in my way.

Poor, harmless old man, they thought!

That amused me, as it always will. Little did they know of the power in my mind, of the activity of which I am capable. Little did they know that I, above all others, organised the system of infiltration in Belgium and Holland, Norway and Denmark, France—and for that matter England—which resulted in the early collapse of the first four countries.

There was little in the streets to surprise me. The people walked quickly. Many were dressed poorly, and most looked pale and strained. They would realise the difference between a France which had controlled its own destiny and a France which was a colony of the Third Reich.

Outside many of the stores were long queues.

Mostly these people made way for me. There appeared to be a dull, apathetic manner in them—all they were interested in was food. There were as many men as women, and the men, I saw, were always at the back of the queue. I noted that fact without realising why.

The windows of the stores were almost empty.

As I neared *l'Hôtel Berliner,* however, there was a shop which was open. Outside this there was a crowd some eight times as big as that outside the others. Too many people had gathered together; the police should have made sure that they were not allowed to congregate in such numbers. Apparently they had tried.

A dozen gendarmes, together with a number of men in civil clothes—men I recognised as German, and doubtless the Gestapo agents with which France was inundated so as to maintain order—advanced towards the queue. I heard much shouting, but I did not clearly understand what was being said. These sheep, I thought, will move on directly a gendarme's white truncheon was drawn; they will not risk the use of revolvers.

But I was wrong.

The crowd overflowed into the road even as far as the opposite pavement. It made little difference to road traffic, for there was virtually none; I had seen only one private car and three hospital ambulances since leaving the hotel.

The shouting took on an uglier note.

I realised then why the men were at the rear of the queue; they were there deliberately to prevent the women being driven away from the shop. I saw a gendarme raise his truncheon indeterminately, and then four or five men threw themselves at him. In a moment he was on the ground amid a flurry of arms and legs. It was the signal for a general rush, and to my anger I saw many of the Gestapo men turn and hurry out of sight.

But some remained, and drew their guns. Bullets were fired into the crowd.

113

In principle I agreed with that, for there was nothing else the Gestapo men could do; the crowd must be taught who was master.

Yet the bullets came my way, for I was one of the crowd.

17

Riot

The situation was not easy to describe.

Only one who has been in my position could understand it. Helpless, with only Joachim to assist me, I was surrounded by shouting, swearing, fighting men. Bullets—a few dozen desultory ones at first—were fired high, although I saw one man hit in the face, and fall down screaming.

Joachim pushed where he could find gaps.

It was useless for me to switch on the motor, for I would be jammed up against a wall of enraged men and thus be unable to move forward, and they would turn on me. I began to sweat. I was afraid that they would know who I was.

They had cause to hate me.

My breathing grew difficult. I heard the shooting grow more frequent, and then above the din of the crowd heard the rasp of motor-engines, the deep roar of military vehicles.

The military had come at last to restore order.

But I had to get out of the crowd before a regular volley was fired.

Not until then did I realise how well the crowd was prepared. I was first startled by the sight of a man with an army revolver in his hand. He drew from his pocket a belt of ammunition and slung it over his shoulder. And others were armed with all manner of weapons: there were even old carbines and shotguns which must have been used in the French Revolution.

Bullets flew both ways.

I forgot my danger.

114

I do not say that boastfully; it is a fact. I forgot that a chance bullet might at any moment strike me. I was appalled by what I was experiencing. I could understand food riots; hunger will drive men temporarily mad and if a few are killed as a result, then there is more food for the rest although the fools do not realise it. The British blockade, so ineffective in some ways, was affecting these people badly, just as it was other countries in Europe. I have read suggestions that the food should be equally distributed, on 'humanitarian' grounds. *Ach,* the fools who suggest it should be shot. The chosen people must be fed, the army of the Fatherland cannot have short rations, the great multitude of armament workers must be kept strong. If there is hunger amongst the subject nations, let them learn to grow more food, or to eat less. The French have over-eaten for many years.

No, a food riot did not disturb me.

But this was more than a riot. It was an organised revolt.

I owed my immunity to Joachim.

In some miraculous way he steered the chair through the crowd. Some made way for me, I remember. There was a narrow alley between two shops, outside which three or four men were standing—and then I saw another disquieting thing.

Along the alley, which led to courtyards at the rear of the shop, the women of the queue had gathered. They must have moved swiftly and by a well-organised arrangement. They were out of danger there. Nothing subdues men more quickly than the knowledge that their womenfolk will suffer—so these women were protected. The instigators had left nothing to chance.

I heard a crash of shots.

I thought at first that it was a volley from the military, but as I turned my head I saw that it was directed from the rioters, many of whom had taken up positions in doorways. From the windows, furniture—yes, and sandbags!—had been thrown, and barricades were hurriedly erected, a big one outside the shop which had been open. Other doors were opened then, and gave security to the insurgents.

It was done with a frightening efficiency.

Two lorry-loads of troops had arrived but stopped at

115

the far end of the street. Sandbags were thrown from another lorry, and barricades were also made for them. I was filled with an alarm which had nothing to do with my personal danger, or with my search for Mondel, my battle of wits with von Stroem

The soldiers had anticipated the need for such precautions!

When I had first seen the mob I had believed that a well-directed volley would scatter them. I now knew that was not the case, the fight would last for some hours. Even worse, such organised revolts were frequent or they could not have been so carefully prepared.

After the one outburst, the shooting remained desultory. I did not need much telling that the military—Frenchmen I saw—had no heart for this. Worse—their heart was probably with the rioters. It appeared to me that if the country were left to the protection of its own army it would soon be in open revolt.

I pulled Joachim down to me, and whispered:

'We must get out, Joachim.'

'At the earliest opportunity, Excellency.'

'We must make one,' I said. 'We must have this settled once and for all, Joachim. There are detachments of our troops fifty miles to the north—they must be despatched here.'

'It is "unoccupied territory", Excellency. That is doubtless the difficulty.'

'Do I need to be told that?' I snapped at him. 'But if it were generally known that the situation were as bad as this, then it would not be unoccupied much longer. This must be crushed. A curse on Petain, he is ruling from here!'

'I will try to find a way out, Excellency,' said Joachim.

He spent many years in France during the war of 1914–18, and had picked up much of the local *patois*. True it was from further north, but it sounded real enough to people anywhere in France, and he excluded the guttural tone in his natural speaking voice. He stepped forward and spoke to a big ruffian who was behind a table that had been lowered from the windows. I saw the ruffian turn, and there was a muttered consultation.

The big man shrugged, and nodded,

Joachim came hurrying back to me, his eyes showing his pleasure at having been successful.

I was surprised at the silence which had fallen on the crowd. That might have been because the military were so inefficient—the swine would not make a determined effort to dislodge the rioters. But I gained the impression that the latter were waiting for something, the nature of which I could not guess.

On the sidewalk, where Joachim pushed me—guards at the barricades made no effort to prevent my progress—I saw that the shops were being looted methodically. It appeared as if everything which they contained was being brought out; not only foodstuffs. There was an amazing miscellany of small barrows, perambulators and handcarts, brought from somewhere, thus providing further evidence of prearrangement, and these were being carefully loaded.

The comparative silence was uncanny.

But the work proceeded so smoothly that I knew that in some measure the *poilus* hiding like cowards behind their lorries were collaborating. There should have been a far stronger force, and approach should have been made from both ends of the street.

Once I reached *l'Hôtel Berliner* I would alter that!

I did not immediately get that far, although I reached the end of the street and saw why no attack came from there. It was barricaded to a height of six feet, with only two small gaps for pedestrians. These gaps were strongly fortified and guarded.

As I reached one, a sentry stood aside—an unshaven man and small, a typical *apache* with a dirty cigarette dangling from his lips. He actually winked at me.

'We do not need the cripples,' he said, and I clenched my teeth, although Joachim smiled at him and thanked him. Joachim began to push me through, but as we reached the opening someone came from the other side.

A shortish, bulky man, unshaven, fair-headed, rudely disguised but enough to protect him from anyone who did not know him well. *I* knew who it was—*I* knew that Fuller was being admitted to this little section of Vichy which for the moment was controlled by insurgent French!

■   ■   ·   ■   ■

117

If only I could have known of it before.

I would have gone on despite the bullets and the danger, for I would have been far safer among them than with Fuller. He was speaking to a tall, clean-shaven Frenchman, the first man that morning who was in any way well groomed, but he looked ahead of him suddenly, and he saw me.

He stopped short.

Doing so he knocked against his companion, who staggered to one side and then said in some surprise:

'What is it, my friend? Have you been stung?'

'Yes,' said Fuller, still staring at me. 'I have been stung, there are too many poisonous reptiles in Vichy.'

His companion regarded him with surprise.

'You joke, my friend!'

Fuller could not disguise his eyes; no man can, except to alter their shape a little by stitching at the corners, and then the stitching is visible unless it is completed by an operation which makes the disguise a permanent one.

Nor did he try to disguise his naked hatred of me.

I saw Joachim move his hand towards his pocket.

If Joachim drew his gun it meant that he would have to make an effort to break through the opening in the barricade, and the danger would be considerable. Joachim had stepped forward to my side, or I could not have seen him. I touched his leg with my left arm, in warning. His hand remained in his pocket.

All this I saw out of the corner of my eye: I continued to watch Fuller narrowly.

Never have I been so completely in one man's power. If he mentioned my name the crowd would fall upon me. Some fool had arranged for the publication of my 'life story' after my retirement, and no one in Europe was unaware of my achievements.

I would be torn limb from limb, for the French can hate, and they do not forget.

But then Fuller said: 'I was joking, my friend. Let us permit the invalid to pass.'

I was to go through, he had some reason for not disclosing my identity. I did not realise why he did it then, all I knew was that he was making the mistake, vital for me.

118

I was too relieved even to estimate the situation properly, and as I went through, Fuller passed me.

As he went, I heard a great cry.

It must have been from a thousand voices, not from one—and it was not anger, it was a greeting, spontaneous and wild. At first I was puzzled, and then I knew that the rioters were greeting Fuller, and I knew also for whom they had been waiting.

He was their hero!

18

The Jewess Again

I have read again that preceding chapter before commencing this.

I have endeavoured to present the circumstances as they occurred, but I do not think that I have properly transmitted the cold horror with which I saw it all. The riot, at first, had worried me chiefly because I was involved in it, but the calm and unhurried developments had a different effect altogether.

No regular army could have moved with greater precision.

I had not fully appreciated the fact of the six-feet high barrier across one end of the street, but I did so more as I went through, and saw that the traffic in the road beyond was proceeding normally. It was a main thoroughfare, I forget its name. There was some motor traffic on it, a great number of cyclists, and some horse-drawn vehicles. But the appalling thing was that they passed as if nothing was the matter. Even gendarmes were standing by idly, and I recognised sight-seeing German soldiers.

German soldiers!

My stomach turned.

They were traitors, they were worse than the accursed French themselves! They must have heard the shooting and known what was happening, but they appeared quite unconcerned.

119

Then—then there was Fuller.

I knew what the roar of welcome meant. He was leading them, was their accepted leader. Whether they thought him to be a Frenchman or not I do not know. I do know that he spoke French to the well-groomed, clean-shaven man, and that he sounded like a native.

Murdoch and Fuller, Dell and Angell were behind the uprising; they had somehow contrived to get arms for the rabble. Small wonder Fuller and Murdoch had been able to move about with such freedom.

But even then it was a fantastic achievement.

What were the authorites doing?

I could understand, perhaps, if the Petain Government sympathised and allowed these things to happen unchecked, but what were the German advisers doing? Why was Berchtesgarten not informed?

Had von Stroem known how bad the situation was?

I thought with some confusion over what he had said and what Murdoch had told me. Something of Murdoch's statement had been true. France *was* ripe for revolution. I had thought that any rising would be easily quelled because the people had no arms. But if they had obtained some, they could obtain others.

I must see von Stroem without losing time, and he must explain what had happened to make such a situation possible.

My mouth was dry as I reached the other hotel.

The normalcy of everything there was appalling. Two commissionaires came hurrying, and opened the doors wide for me to be wheeled through. The foyer was as busy as it must have been in peacetime. Three clerks were at the desk, and at least forty people were in the foyer-lounge.

Joachim knew von Stroem's room.

He pushed me towards the lift, and as we reached it the doors were opened by a boy to allow three people to step out. Two of them were middle-aged Jews, and my gorge rose. The third was young and beautiful. I saw her fine breast and then looked into her bold, dark eyes.

She was Mitzi Weiner, von Stroem's mistress.

The older Jews bowed and hurriedly stepped out of my way.

Mitzi Weiner did not immediately move. She looked down at me, and inclined her head.

'Good morning, Herr Horst.'

I forced myself to be civil.

'Good morning, Fräulein. You found your parents?'

'You have just seen them,' she said, and I think she was smiling because she knew that I had disbelieved her. It even went through my mind that I should order her detention. I think I would have done, but for the riot outside.

In Germany and Austria, to name a Jew was to have him or her arrested. I had thought by then that France had been taught to understand that was essential under the New Order. But now I doubted—yes, I doubted!—whether I could have her detained simply by saying she was a Jewess. I was not sure of the strength of the authorities. I knew—I can never explain how sick the knowledge made me—that in Vichy, if not in the rest of France, there was an effective resistance organisation on the lines of those which I had built up so often.

I decided suddenly to say nothing to the Jewess. I could find her when I wanted her.

'Forward, Joachim,' I said, and actually started the wheel myself, so that my chair brushed against her thigh. I glared up and round at her, and I heard her say in her throaty voice:

'A thousand apologies, Herr Horst.'

There was a mirror in the lift, and in it I saw her go to her parents—*were* they her parents? Could there be any possibility that she was not von Stroem's mistress?

I put that thought aside; Elsa had confirmed it.

von Stroem's apartment was on the first floor, and the door was opened as I reached it. I saw Elsa standing in the first room, and von Stroem was looking down on her with his lips twisted. He was very pale. The wound on his cheek was covered with a plaster patch which had become loose.

'Either I have to endure it being loose, or have my face swathed in bandages.' Apart from that he had no other greeting for me, but pressed a bell push. A nurse entered—

121

a middle-aged woman with short grey hair who wore glasses which did nothing to conceal a bad squint.

'Refix this, please,' said von Stroem.

The nurse took the plaster patch off quickly—they will never be careful, but perhaps a quick pain is best—and I saw the ugly wound. The groove of the bullet was quite clear; it was near the right cheekbone. The flesh had been torn in other places, and there were three sutures. The whole of the right side of his face was red with inflammation which had spread to his eye.

He was a different man from the one I had seen the previous day; his manner with the nurse was irritable, and twice he cursed her, although she continued with her work swiftly and neatly. She had brought a fresh dressing and more plaster, and when she had finished it she said:

'If you insist on talking it will loosen again.'

'I will talk as I wish!' snarled von Stroem. 'Have you never been taught to know your place?'

The nurse's lips tightened. She was French, of course. She glared at von Stroem with scarcely-veiled hostility before leaving. It was clear that the night had affected von Stroem badly. His hands shook when he lit a cigarette. But he made a considerable effort to control himself.

'We will go into my room,' he said.

He stood aside for me to enter first. I did not allow Joachim to push me, but with his help rose from my chair, and rested on my stick while I found my balance. Then I stumped slowly through into the big room beyond.

No one else was there.

Elsa and von Stroem followed, and Joachim stayed in the small room.

On the previous day von Stroem had been a man in rude health, quite certain of himself, poised and—as I have often remarked—gloating over my infirmity. Now *he* was a sick man, or thought he was.

He sat down in an easy chair. I decided to remain standing.

'Well, von Stroem,' I said, 'you have much to explain. Why was I not told of the situation in Vichy?'

He lifted his hand.

'What does it signify? There is a small band of men who

122

believe they are well-organised. They do not grow to un-wieldly numbers. They prepare occasional *coups* such as I understand you witnessed this morning, they loot a little, and they go away. Nothing more is heard of them for weeks. It has happened so often that it is not considered important any more.'

'*I* consider it important,' I declared. 'von Stroem, you gave me the flimsiest of details, only some of which were accurate. It is regrettable. Since my arrival here I have seen Murdoch and one of his men. They have much power in the district.'

'You have *seen* them?'

'I could have detained them,' I said irritably, 'but it is Mondel, not Murdoch, whom we want. When we have Mondel we can do what we like with Murdoch.' I believed that to be true, and certainly I was not going to give the full facts to this man—a man of mystery who was cracking so fast! 'I wish several things done at once—Schlesser should be in a position to arrange them. He will send word from Paris.'

'What are they?' demanded von Stroem. But I was no longer prepared to accept orders or advice from this man.

'The manager of *l'Hôtel Grande* is a spy,' I stated. 'He must be detained and questioned. I have reason to believe that he allowed Fuller to enter my room last night. Then there is a woman—a Jewess named Weiner. She must also be detained.'

I said that casually, since ordering the detention of a Jewess was the most ordinary thing in the world—but I saw his hands tighten, and I thought for a moment that he would betray himself.

He did not.

'What has she done?' he asked.

'She has acted suspiciously.'

'In what way?' He spoke quietly; too quietly.

'She forced entry into my apartment last night.'

'You appear to have had quite a number of visitors,' he sneered, but I did not let him have much satisfaction.

'I control my visitors, von Stroem. These matters are details but must be attended to at once. Arrange for the detentions. Schlesser will confirm them from Paris.'

'I will do it soon,' he said.

'Now!' I insisted.

That demand was the final test.

If he refused I did not see how I could make him obey. I believed that he would arrange for the hotel manager's detention but that he wanted to give Mitzi Weiner time to get away. His answer would confirm or deny my degree of authority over him.

There was silence, and a tension it is not easy to explain. And then slowly he reached out for the telephone.

I glanced at him, and then at Elsa, who was looking my way. Triumph was in our eyes, for we knew we had him where we wanted him! It was strange that he should have disintegrated so easily, although my mention of the woman Weiner must have given him a severe shock.

He called the *Commissariat de Police,* gave his name, and then his orders. Apparently no query was raised, but he made a mistake which was unbelievable.

He gave Mitzi Weiner's address at the hotel, thus proving that he knew it!

What had happened to the man? I did not believe that the shooting had disturbed his morale so severely; something else had happened, something which made him afraid. He finished telephoning, then turned and said in snort, jerky sentences:

'von Horssell, there are disturbing factors. It has been discovered that Mondel has been in touch with representatives of Free France. I did not know it—the discovery was made abroad. The tone of his newspapers has been unsatisfactory today. He has evaded all reference to the wisdom of co-operating with the Reich. He is somewhere not far from Vichy, I believe—and he personally is conducting his editorials. On instructions from Berchtesgarten the papers were not confiscated. It is believed better that it should be thought that in Friday's interview he shall have been converted.'

I said: 'That is good policy. But I am at a loss to understand the man's influence. The interview with the Leader can be printed, as I have said before—and if he transmits the wrong leading articles—*ach,* they can be rewritten.'

von Stroem shook his head.

124

His right eye was half-closed, and he would have been a laughable spectacle but for the seriousness of the matter we were discussing. I understood more of his anxiety now. The Leader had learned something of his failure; he was afraid that orders would come for his return to Berchtesgarten, and he had reason enough to be afraid.

'It cannot be done so easily,' he said.

'*Ach,* has your wound robbed you of a mind?' I rasped. 'von Stroem, the articles will be printed as we wish, not as Mondel or his printers and editors wish.'

'Then no papers would be published,' he declared. 'And a strike would tell the people of estrangement between the Reich and Mondel. You must understand how well he has exerted his influence. And . . .' He stood up and paced the room, speaking as he walked. 'Excellency, there is this factor of importance. In order to make sure that the leading articles appear as he has written them, Mondel has for some time past issued copies, in leaflet form. The distribution of these leaflets is widespread, and cannot be stopped. They are sometimes duplicated sheets, sometimes printed, sometimes written by hand. To convince the people of the genuineness of the coming interview, it must *be* genuine. Once we find Mondel we can force him to act as we wish, but we must get him!'

I leaned back against the wall.

I wished I were in my chair instead of standing, for that statement was one which nearly frightened me. The widespread distribution of leaflets, secretly printed—how comprehensive *was* this organisation which Mondel had built up?

I said: 'We will get Mondel.'

'Then how?' he flashed. 'I do not hide from you that it worries me. I cannot trace him. I have used every man and every method I know. I have thrown a thousand people into camps. I have executed others, I have been looking for Mondel for more than a month! My life, my whole career, is at stake. The man is more elusive than Otto Strasser was in Berlin! Do you realise you have forty-eight hours, not only to find him but to reduce him to a state of mind in which he will humble himself before the Leader?'

I rasped: 'Your life and career are unimportant. The

triumph of the Third Reich matters. We will get Mondel.'

He almost shrieked: 'But how?'

But I was as empty of ideas as he.

19

I Purge Vichy

I did not allow von Stroem to know that.

I looked at him expressionlessly, knowing that he was waiting on my words. I took a step forward—*thump!*—a pause—*thump!* I did that deliberately, and made him start; certainly he was in a fine state of nerves. Whatever message he had received from Berchtesgarten must have turned his heart within him.

I said: 'I shall not discuss it now. I have seen Murdoch, and I know that Murdoch can lead us to Mondel. I can find Murdoch whenever I wish.'

He stared as if he did not believe me.

'How? Do you know where he is?'

'I know what will bring him to me,' I said harshly. 'But first, Vichy must be purged of traitors and rebels.'

'The—the city is in a bad way,' he said, proving that he had lied when he had made light of it earlier. 'It will not be easy.'

'In three hours we can have ten thousand troops here,' I thundered. 'In five we can have mechanised units, tanks, machine-guns—everything we need. In one'—I lowered my voice then, and was almost gentle—'in one night the city can be bombed until the people behave like frightened rats.'

'But—but we are not at war with France!'

'You thrice-damned fool!' I roared. 'We are at war. The armistice is but an armistice, no peace treaty has been signed. And if it had, what then? The French authorities have allowed its capital to get out of hand. They have broken all the clauses of the armistice treaty—*Gott in himmel,* must I talk to you as a child. Call Berchtes-garten!'

He hesitated. 'But Baron . . .'

I moved then. I did not realise that I had the power, but I went forward more swiftly than I have moved for a long time without the serum, thumping down first my stick and then my left foot. I reached the telephone, and with my right hand I snatched it up. I thought the withered fingers would drop it, but Elsa came quickly to prevent it falling.

The operator spoke: I gave the fearful number.

'At once, at once, Excellency,' said the operator.

von Stroem was breathing very heavily—much as I breathe at times. He did not try to touch the telephone, but said:

'Baron, you cannot give those orders by telephone. They will be all over the city before the message is finished. I have been up all night discussing the situation. It is worse by far than I had feared. Before aeroplanes arrived they would be in full revolt . . .'

'They will be bombed to pieces!' I snarled.

I had intended to ask permission to speak to the Führer himself, and I believe he would have listened to me. I had proposed telling him the situation, and to request his authority for my purge. But I decided it would be wiser to ask for an interview. I could fly to Berchtesgarten and back in no more than eight hours.

'But, you fool,' I said to von Stroem, 'do you imagine that I propose to talk of matters which any spy can over-hear?'

I was glad that in my rage at his impotence I had not risked talking on the telephone of what I proposed to do. It was not the first time I had ordered such a purge, but in the past I had full authority. *I* ordered the onslaught on Rotterdam.

There was a silence broken only by heavy breathing, and then a fresh voice came onto the telephone.

.   .

I am but a man.

I knew that voice the moment I heard it, and I showed the consternation which it wrought in me. I had heard it a million times in my mind, but on those occasions I had been lying awake and expecting it, even answering its questions.

On the telephone I had not dreamed of hearing it.

I think I had forgotten Murdoch and Mary Dell. My mind was wholly with the problem of arranging for the complete subjection of the city by the one means which could ensure swift and proper results.

von Stroem had seemed aghast at the thought of bombing, but fifty 'planes in ten minutes could teach the scum such a lesson that they would not dare complain nor protest when a general purge was ordered. The mechanised columns and the troops would occupy the city—ostensibly 'passing through'. What do words mean?

I hoped in a few minutes to speak to the Leader himself, or at least to one of the Party leaders. Instead I heard a woman's voice, low-pitched and possessing a hint of laughter—*Gott in himmel,* the laughter of Murdoch and Dell is a thing I will never understand!

Murdoch I could have understood. But it was Mary Dell, and I believe she was speaking from the hotel itself.

She said to me: 'Good morning, Baron. How is Elsa?'

I do not think she could have caused a greater sensation in my mind had she said:

'Hitler is dead and Berlin has capitulated.'

I was aware of Elsa, standing rigid; of von Stroem eyeing me strangely. My throat constricted. My right side became suddenly weak, and I cursed the fact that I had not stayed in my chair. I felt the perspiration at my forehead and my neck, and the swelling of my veins as the blood welled into them.

Neither of the others spoke.

But from the telephone Mary Dell said:

'You're breathing heavily, aren't you? Have you been hurrying? Old men should be careful, you know, arteries can harden.' She paused, and then as if she were talking to someone near her I heard her voice: *'What's that? Yes, darling, the old idiot is still there. He's recovering from the shock.'*

A man's voice followed, indistinctly, and I heard him laugh. The woman said: *'Be quiet, Bruce.'*

So Murdoch was with her.

Where—what part of the town or the hotel?

I placed a hand over the telephone mouthpiece and said in an urgent whisper to Elsa and von Stroem:

'Dell is here, perhaps in the hotel. Find out where.'

Elsa acted very quickly on my words, although von Stroem hesitated, and she had to call him. I removed my hand, and in a voice which gave little sign of my consternation I answered her:

'It is my habit to breathe heavily.'

'I know you and your habits,' she said, and added with a change of tone: 'Didn't you ask for a number, Baron?'

'For now you may prevent me getting it. Afterwards . . .'

'Afterwards,' she interrupted, 'you won't be very interested. But if the number you wanted was out of the city, you can't have it. Hadn't you heard? There were many mysterious explosions last night, and all the long-distance telephone cables were broken.'

I thought immediately of radio, but I did not say that. I wanted to keep her on the other end of the line until Elsa and von Stroem had had time to investigate, and I said:

'There will be an end to mysterious explosions.'

'Now, now,' chided Mary Dell. 'That is wishful thinking. I did all I could to get you here, but I didn't expect you so soon. Didn't you guess?'

'Guess what?' I rasped.

'You are growing old,' she said. 'My dear Baron, Bruce knew the one thing which would get you here would be mention of us. We went to great trouble to persuade von Stroem to think that the only person we feared was your august self. That worked very well, didn't it?'

'And why did you want me?' I demanded. I did not mind much what was discussed. The words were intended only to keep her there.

'We simply wanted you here,' she said. 'That's all. Old scores, Baron. You are too dangerous a man to be allowed to live, we would rather have you dead than retired.'

'Ach,' I said, speaking my thoughts aloud, 'you could have killed me—Fuller, Murdoch—and again Fuller this morning. Why did he let me go?'

'I wonder,' she said. 'He would have a reason, Baron, I'll ask him about it. I . . .' She broke off, and my heart leapt with the hope that Elsa or von Stroem had reached her, but her voice was calm when she spoke to someone near her. 'Good work—you've got them both?'

'Both,' came a man's voice faintly.

'I'm coming up to see you,' said Mary Dell to me, and then she closed her end of the telephone.

She meant to see *me*, of course.

I was alone. My leg had lost what little strength it had. My call to Berchtesgarten could not be made. She had said 'you've got them both' and only a fool would have failed to realise that she meant Elsa and von Stroem.

I replaced the telephone, which slipped at the last moment from my withered hand, and clattered noisily: I left it on the table. I leaned forward for my stick, and contrived to get my balance with it. My chair was not ten feet away from me, but appeared to be a mile or more.

I croaked: 'Joachim—come in, Joachim.'

There was no response. So they had him too.

Nor was there a bell communicating with the next room, even had he been there to answer, and I had to reach the chair myself. I stood quite still for some seconds, then laboriously moved forward. My hand trembled as I put my weight on my stick.

I was no more than halfway to my chair when the door opened.

I did not hope it was Elsa or von Stroem, or even Joachim. I knew that such a hope would be in vain. I looked therefore at Mary Dell as she came in, and at the tall thin man beyond her.

That was Angell.

He had his left arm in a sling, obviously where he had been wounded when escaping from the grounds of my house. How long ago that seemed! How differently had I imagined the course of events after they had gone in the car. How little I had dreamed that instead of being able to direct operations I would be forced on the defensive.

They had given me no rest.

They had actually *wanted* me here, had tricked von Stroem into getting me here. The thought had not been originally his—oh, I believed Mary Dell! I knew she would not lie without a purpose, and there would be none in lying about that.

She had not changed greatly.

In fact I noticed only two different things about her. Her hair was cut short at the back—the term, I believe, is 'shingle-bob'—and there was a slight red mark on the bridge of her nose. That told me two things: that when she was disguised she wore a wig, and also glasses.

Her hair was tossed back carelessly from her broad forehead and her eyes were laughing at me, deep blue and hateful. She can speak volumes with her eyes. Her wide and shapely mouth was curved a little, and on her cheeks there was the bloom of health.

Why should I not admit that?

With Murdoch she had performed a virtual miracle. In a country controlled by the Fatherland, with a puppet-Government which in most things did exactly what was ordered, they had sown the seeds of revolt and unrest until in places and for a time they could take control. One could almost call it 'peaceful penetration'—that weapon of the Leader's which he has so often used to good effect.

Oh, they were clever.

And more than that; I shall never be able to understand them.

The smile faded from the woman's eyes when she saw me. Angell, who has a large and somewhat humorous face, although good-looking in its way, frowned as if unpleasantly surprised. Both stepped forward, and the firm grip of Mary Dell's hand on my arm might have been Elsa's.

She helped me into my chair without speaking.

Angell also helped, and I was too glad of the rest to protest, although I would have given much to be able to do everything myself. Sitting down, however, with my leg stretched in front of me, I was much easier. There was a mirror on the wall and I could see myself when Mary Dell moved aside.

There was no colour in my lips or my cheeks. My face was set, but I thought myself to be looking at a death's head mask made in macabre mockery of my living self. I understood the change in their manner much better. I longed

131

for coffee, but as I could get none I looked at the water decanter on a table behind Angell.

The woman understood my meaning, poured out a glass of water and held it to my lips. I took it roughly with my left hand, which is in perfect order as she knew well, and spilled a little on my coat and trousers. The water was cold and refreshing.

'I am obliged,' I said hoarsely.

'I thought you were going to run out on us,' said Mary Dell in a more sober voice.

'I have much to do before I die,' I rasped.

'Yes,' said Mary, and she sat against a table, while Angell took an easy chair and stretched out his long legs. 'You hope you have,' she added. 'von Horssell, don't you realise what this means?'

'It means I have more to do than I thought,' I replied.

She lifted her hands, as if she could not understand my spirit or my confidence in myself.

'One man and woman out of every five in Vichy is with us,' she declared. 'The staff of this hotel is nearly all pro-British—so are the staffs at many other hotels. The Vichy Government is rife with the same spirit—ministers as well as clerks. The organised food-rioting is kept within bounds only because we desire it that way. You cannot telephone, you are not likely to be able to use a radio. The airfields are staffed with mechanics and gendarmes who are with us. Did you know that, Baron von Horssell?'

'It has become obvious,' I said with an effort.

'Obvious,' she echoed. 'Yes, it is obvious all right. Elsa and von Stroem are with Bruce now, and he won't be well-disposed towards them.'

'Well, what of that?' I demanded.

'You are quite helpless,' she reminded me.

'That is your mistake!' I rasped.

And for the first time since I had heard her voice I believed it. I knew suddenly why I had not been killed, why Fuller had allowed me to go that morning. I should have seen the truth before but it had escaped me.

They wanted help from me.

That was why I had been brought to Vichy. That explained a great many things, perhaps even the fact that the bullets in the grounds of my house had not taken effect. Murdoch and Dell had wanted me here, had written to Elsa and contrived those other things to make sure that even if I refused to make the journey for political reasons, I would for the purpose of vengeance. They understood me well enough for that.

The knowledge gave me fresh strength and hope.

I did not know what they could possibly want, but it would be something of great importance, and if I could pretend to tell them I might get an opportunity to free myself and send word to Berchtesgarten.

Mary Dell leaned forward, her hands in the tiny cross-cut pockets of her skirt. She had on a black coat and a high-necked yellow blouse.

'But we will do a deal with you,' she said. 'We will let you go, with Elsa and Joachim, in exchange for one item of information.'

'What is it?' I rasped.

'It's very simple,' said Mary Dell, and she drew her hands from her pockets and stood up. 'We want to know where Mondel is, nothing more. We want Mondel in exchange for your safety, Baron. That is all.'

20

Where is Mondel?

That was *all*!

Murdoch did not know where Mondel was!

It was fortunate that I had been given time to compose myself, and that I had suspected before she had spoken that she wanted to come to terms on a matter so important that I had been allowed to go free when I could so easily have been killed.

Mary Dell wanted to know where Mondel was—that was *all*! I would have given ten million marks to have known! *Murdoch did not know.*

133

I had not yet fully grasped the importance of Mondel. That, of course, was because I had not realised how weak was our control of occupied France. But the realisation was growing fast, and although I had no evidence beyond what I had been told I now knew that to Murdoch and Dell, Mondel was of the greatest importance. Dell—Mondel. Could there be any significance in that?

Of course not. I mention the point only to demonstrate that despite the problems confronting me I was able to think coolly and dispassionately.

'Well?' asked Angell sharply.

It was the first time he had spoken since he had entered, and I looked at him coldly.

'You are bigger fools than I thought,' I said. 'Surely you do not imagine that I will bargain with facts of importance to the Reich for my personal safety.'

'Oh, no,' said Mary Dell, 'we didn't expect it, Baron, we just tried it out. We shall leave you to think about it. I'm sorry that we can't send Joachim to you, but you can have a nurse if you wish.'

'I shall be obliged,' I said.

'She squints,' said Mary Dell.

One of the irritating and at times worrying things about her as well as Murdoch is the abrupt way in which they behave. I would have handled the situation very differently. I would have spent an hour talking, threatening, even causing pain—pain will make the most unexpected people speak. I knew of course that no matter what they did they could not get the information from me, for I did not know it. Even had I known, I would have endured the tortures of the damned before I told.

But I *could* lie.

They gave me no opportunity, but one would come. I watched the door close behind them and saw Angell turn back, look into the room, and purse his lips to make an absurd rasping sound.

The fool!

When the door closed I shut my eyes, then opened them slowly and looked into the mirror. I had regained a little of my colour. I wished for one thing more than any other— that I could have one hour of normal activity. The serum was always invaluable; just then it would have been ten times more important.

I wondered how long the nurse would be.

I had heard the key turn in the lock, a precaution I would have taken myself, in spite of the fact that they knew I could not move. I shifted in my chair, wondering how soon Murdoch or Dell would come again. Oddly enough now that I was working against them and had seen them in the flesh and the blood the depth of hatred which I had felt for them before had lessened. I considered them as ciphers, not as human beings.

If Joachim were here, he might have the serum—or Elsa would. Elsa carried it, usually in her handbag when we were busy. The serum and a syringe.

I stared at the table beneath the mirror, and I felt my breath constricting because of what I saw. I looked, and closed my eyes, and looked again—and then I knew it was no figment of my imagination, but a fact.

Elsa's bag was on the table!

She had gone out hurriedly, of course, and I knew she carried a small automatic in the pocket of her coat, so that there had been no reason for her to take her bag. I did not know for certain that the serum or the syringe was inside, but at least there was a chance.

I wheeled my chair to the table.

Although I was almost afraid of opening the bag and finding the serum missing, I did not hesitate but took it and unfastened the clasp. There was a variety of oddments at the top—a powder compact, a handkerchief, a notebook. I pulled them out quickly, putting them on the table. Then I drew a deep breath and my heart beat tumultuously

The serum was there!

It was in a small box with the syringe—I know it as well as I know my own face. I drew it out, and then burst into a cold sweat, for the nurse might come at any moment and she would doubtless be told to report anything unusual. I remembered then her manner with von Stroem, and had wondered that she dared talk so to a high German official.

Gott in himmel, did that matter?

I replaced the oddments from the bag which I put back where I had found it. I opened the box, taking out the serum and the syringe—but only the syringe was necessary. Elsa had left nothing to chance, and the syringe was filled and ready.

My ears were strained to catch the slightest sound as I fumbled with the flap in the thigh of my trousers and bared the wrinkled flesh. I took the syringe—and then I heard footsteps approaching, the light footsteps of a woman.

I pressed the plunger.

I emptied the needle and withdrew it. I was already preparing to put both box and syringe into my pocket when the footsteps passed the door, and I knew that I was temporarily reprieved. More carefully I replaced the equipment, and then I put the box at the bottom of Elsa's bag again. If by chance I was searched and the things were discovered Murdoch would know what I had done, for he had once shot the instrument from my hand to prevent me from using it.

I felt the strength coursing through my body.

My right side was alive with a constant prickle of pain that was almost unbearable, and the whole of my body was sweating. It was far worse than when I had used the serum on the previous day; my medical adviser tells me that at most I should use it once each month.

But the pain subsided at last.

I began to ease myself from my chair, and again the miracle of transformation was accomplished, for when I placed my right foot on the ground it supported me. But before I stepped from the chair I heard footsteps again, and was reminded that the nurse must be coming before long.

I sat back.

There was a scratch at the door, that of a key being pushed in, and then the door opened to admit the nurse. I had a fear that she might not be alone, but I need not have concerned myself. Why should Murdoch and Dell suspect that anything more than a nurse was needed for a helpless old man?

Old man! I had to stop myself from laughing.

I saw why she had been so long in coming, and why she had fumbled a little at the door, for she was carrying a tray of coffee. I wonder what is in people like Murdoch or Dell to make such gestures.

136

The nurse apparently had no sympathy with it. Her villainous squint was turned towards me, and I had to repress the temptation to order her to look away.

'They've sent you coffee,' she said in French. 'It is a waste I think—there is too little real coffee in France since you swines of Huns have taken everything.'

I bit on my angry retort.

'And you, you pig, you have nothing to say now, now you are the one to face death. I wish there could be a thousand deaths for you, who have killed thousands! If I had my way you would be killed a little bit each day, for a year—you would be made to know all the pain you have inflicted on the innocent and the helpless.' She poured coffee as she spoke, and there was a vicious hatred in her which I acknowledged and respected.

She held out the coffee, then drew it back.

'It is a long time since *I* have enjoyed coffee,' she said, and for a moment I was afraid that she would keep it away from me. I stared at her, quite expressionless, as if it did not matter, although I needed that stimulant to put the finishing touch to my temporary recovery.

If I protested she might deliberately drink it.

She gave it to me, and I drank the hot beverage gladly, watching her as I did so. All the time she talked, her high-pitched French voice going sometimes to a point of frenzy—how she hated me and all that was German!

Had she been silent, and even sullen, I might not have determined to extort the full price, but I determined to kill her. I drank slowly, watching her, turning over my plan of action in my mind. I would have three-quarters of an hour of free movement, even a little more, once I was out of the room. I would go through the window, of course—if I went through the door and along the passages I might be recognised despite the fact that I was walking, and I knew that *l'Hôtel Berliner* was built on the same plan as *l'Hôtel Grande*.

I finished the coffee, and handed her the cup.

She leaned forward to take it, and my left hand shot out and gripped her wrist. Cup and saucer fell to my knees and then to the carpet, but that did not matter. I pulled her so sharply and gripped her so hard that she gasped with pain, and I then used my right hand to reinforce the left. I placed it about her throat, and my pressure increased so that her cries were silenced abruptly.

I squeezed.

I felt the power that was in me as the pressure tightened, and I wanted to kill her with my right hand, the hand which is so often unable to lift a spoon. But I heard footsteps in the passage and so I released my hold on her and let her fall to the floor. She was unconscious, and her glasses had been dislodged, her hair was not as precisely arranged as when she had entered.

I stood up, grasping my stick.

The footsteps passed. Normal business was proceeding at the hotel despite what was happening outside. I stepped to the door and locked it—the nurse had omitted to do that —and for extra safety put a chair beneath the handle. I did the same to a second door, leading to an ante-room— where I had seen von Stroem and Elsa.

I walked into the bedroom, and in von Stroem's luggage I found a revolver, exactly what I needed. I stepped again to the room where the nurse was lying, on the floor and looking up at me.

'Looking' is not the word; her eyes were partly open, and she had slumped further since I had let her drop.

I put the revolver in my pocket; I should not waste a bullet, and in any case a report would have attracted attention. I leaned down to grip her throat with my hand again —and it was her throat which first attracted my interest. Her stiff collar had been wrenched apart, and she had the slim but full and smooth throat of a young woman.

I looked at her eyes.

I drew a sharp breath as I raised the eyelids so that I could see more clearly, and I knew that I had been deceived —*the nurse did not squint*; the glasses made it appear that she did.

I went very still.

I saw the red ridge on the bridge of her nose, and slowly I pulled at her grey hair; it came away to reveal the dark hair of Mary Dell. Her face was recognisable, too, although cleverly disguised—the more cleverly because it had been done in such a hurry.

Mary Dell, unconscious at my feet, Mary Dell with her
throat beneath my hand. Mary Dell, von Stroem's 'nurse'.
I needed to go no further for the first fruits of revenge.

21

VOSS

Even had the serum not been working within me I believe
that I would have found normal strength in that moment.
I had stood back from her, and was peering past the disguise which she had affected at the person I had known in
England. I admitted that the disguise was given a touch of
genius by the glasses, one lens of which was obviously made
so that it distorted not the vision of the wearer but of the
onlooker. Even had I seen before that a wig was there—and
I had not done, for her starched nurse's veil prevented that
—I would never have dreamed that Mary Dell was actually
in the person of a cross-eyed woman.

The inclination to kill her was strong, but other factors
had to be weighed. If I could take her from the hotel I would
have a hostage to use against Murdoch. I know the man too
well to make any mistake. He would take inordinate risks
to save her, risks which would endanger not only his own
safety but the success of his preparations. Some such hostage was invaluable. Murdoch's position in Vichy was far
too strong, but with the woman in my hands I could at least
gain time. I was able to imagine myself talking to Murdoch
and picturing his face when he realised where Mary Dell's
foolhardiness had taken her. I remember chuckling to myself, sure that I had a means of fighting Murdoch and of
making the odds more even.

But how was I to get her away?

I thought of my chair. I could push it, now, and although
a man in a wheel chair would have been suspect, a woman
in one would not. But how was I to hide her face? Disguised
or not, Murdoch, Angell and probably others would know
her.

I was considering that problem when there was a tap at the door. I started, and looked round over my shoulder, afraid for a moment that it was a courtesy tap only and that the caller would try to open the door immediately. But no —the caller waited.

There was no opportunity of deferring a decision. I gripped Elsa's automatic and I stepped swiftly to the door, cursing myself for having failed to hear the sound of footsteps. I need not have done that, for the caller had come softly and stealthily so as not to attract attention. I unlocked the door and removed the chair, then called: 'Come in.'

I had to do that: if I sent the caller away he—or she—might raise an alarm. In any case I believed that the nurse's voice would be expected in response, and that the caller was perhaps by then suspicious. I stood opposite the door with my gun showing, so that the shock of seeing me, and the fear which would follow, was likely to enjoin silence.

All I needed was to get whoever it was into the room without a noise.

The door opened slowly.

It might have been someone who was nervous of entering, who expected to find danger. I raised my gun . . .

And then abruptly I lowered it.

There are moments when every man will forget himself for a moment, and I did then. I was so surprised—and at the same time relieved—that I called out in a loud voice:

'*Voss!*'

'Be quiet!' he said softly. 'I am not known to be here.'

A servant actually rebuked me!

He came through and closed the door silently behind him, making no sound. Voss is a tall, thin, weedy man. Imagine Crown Prince Wilhelm but a narrower, thinner man and one with an even more vacuous expression, and you see this man. Then he was dressed as a waiter—I had noticed that the French waiters were as impeccable as during the days of peace—and I could not understand why. In fact I could not understand his arrival there at all, but what mattered was the fact that the agent I had summoned to meet me in Vichy had arrived at a moment which could not have been more opportune.

140

Explanations could follow, but one thing I could not fail to comment on to myself. Where every other man and woman who has ever worked for me—except only Elsa—would have been startled to find me on my feet and apparently as hale as they, Voss took it for granted. He has always pleased me because he acts on circumstances as he finds them.

'I will be very quiet,' I said. 'Voss, this is the woman Dell. The hotel is ...'

'I know the situation here,' he said.

'Good. Then you will understand the problem. I want to get her away, but there must be no delay.'

'It is easy,' said Voss, with the air of a man who had performed a conjuring trick professionally. 'I came to get you away, Excellency, with your chair. She can be in it instead.' It was difficult to believe words of such sense coming from this vacant-faced and gangling man, but he acted even as he spoke, and lifted Dell—or began to lift her from the floor. He is not a man of great physical strength, so I helped him, revelling in my ability to do so.

We placed her in the chair, to which was attached a strap for security. Voss fastened this about her waist, and then from the bedroom he brought a blanket and wrapped it about her so that only her shoulders and her head were visible. He took then a pair of smoked glasses from his pocket. They were too large, for he had meant them for me, but they served.

'Excellency, have the goodness to open the door, please, and to see if anyone is in the passage.'

I did so, taking Elsa's bag with me. The passage was empty.

Voss pushed the chair towards me.

'We shall go left,' he said, 'and then through a door which is marked "*femme de chambre*"—it leads to the servants' passage and then the service lift. I have made arrangements for escape that way, Excellency.'

I had no time to congratulate him.

I was on tenterhooks lest someone should come into the passage while we were in it, but there were no interruptions. Three women were busy in the servants' passage, but Voss had clearly paid them to be discreet. There was hardly

141

room in the service lift for the two of us as well as the chair, but by squeezing against the door it was possible for us to travel together.

Voss pressed the button for the ground floor, and while we descended he said quietly:

'I had arranged for a large laundry basket, Excellency—it was all that was possible. Laundry is collected at all hours, none will be surprised to see some going out now. There is a van waiting outside, and another man—ostensibly a porter.'

There was no object in comment from me, except to nod approval, although for some minutes I remained on edge.

I would not have made a similar plan myself, but it worked. There was a large laundry basket—large enough in fact for me!—opposite the lift door on the ground floor, and yet strangely enough no one was in sight but a solid-looking porter. He spoke French, but I judged him to be a German.

Dell was lifted into the basket.

There was room for her to be in a half-sitting position. I was concerned with the possibility that she would regain consciousness, but Voss had not overlooked that. After she was in the basket he tied a scarf about her mouth, forcing it between her jaws so that she would not be able to make any appreciable sound.

The lid was closed, and the basket padlocked.

Voss and the porter between them carried it outside, where a plain van was waiting with a driver at the wheel. I noticed in the narrow street that there were several gendarmes gathered together, as if determined that whatever was happening in the main thoroughfares it was no concern of theirs.

Certainly discipline was needed in Vichy!

But it was no moment for dwelling on that. Once safety had been reached I could consider it urgently, and also find a way of contacting with Berchtesgarten. The possibility was considerably enhanced.

Voss climbed in front with the driver, and I sat on a box with the basket. The doors were closed and the only light came through two small windows let in them. The journey was not comfortable, but I did not complain. Once when rounding a corner I lurched to one side, and the basket

142

slithered across the floor and banged heavily against the bodywork. I thought I heard a faint gasp from inside, and I allowed myself to laugh.

And to think who it was!

She was helpless, she would never be free again. I thought of the dreams I had had, and knew that physical torture would not be so satisfying as to see her face when she realised she was no longer free. The greatest punishment and pain she would know was that I had trapped her; that she would never again see her beloved Murdoch.

I recall that I was surprised when the van stopped. We had not travelled far enough to be beyond the precincts of the city, and subconsciously I had assumed that we would be going outside the city limits. But clearly it was the final stopping place, for there was the noise of men climbing from the front seat, and the engine was cut off.

The doors were opened.

And I saw Joachim!

That was a complete surprise, and one which gave me great pleasure. I had not thought it likely that I would see him again; I had assumed that Murdoch would make sure that he did not escape. Yet Joachim it was, and his face was eager as he spoke in a low-pitched voice—the voice of a man anxious not to be overheard.

'You are well, Excellency?'

'I am,' I said, and then humorously: 'But I did not realise you could drive so carelessly, Joachim!'

'It is the accursed van,' he said. 'I believe that I suffered as much or more than you, Excellency, each time it lurched to one side.'

'We must hurry,' said Voss, and I tolerated his interruption.

Afterwards I learned we were in a residential part of the city where there are many old houses, relics of the prosperous days of France. Many I knew had been turned over to house troops and Gestapo men in Vichy, and it was to one of these that I had been brought. It was broad daylight, but since the van had been brought close to the front door that there was no danger of being seen from the street.

Voss and a man who had come from the house carried the basket in, and I followed with Joachim. He explained,

with his usual care for detail, that he had been taken un-
awares and drugged a few minutes after I had seen von
Stroem, that he had recovered consciousness to find himself in the servants' quarters of the hotel. There was among
the servants a man loyal to the Reich, and Joachim had
been freed; I will not render the precise way in which he
had acted afterwards; it is sufficient to say that after getting
outside he made immediately for *l'Hôtel Grande*.

There he had met Voss.

The loyal man at *l'Hôtel Berliner*, a waiter, had gone
with Joachim. Quickly, it had been arranged that Voss
should return to take his 'duty', while other trustworthy
men had been pressed into service also.

'Whose house is this?' I asked.

I was told it had been taken over by the German authorities, and that some thirty or forty Gestapo men were
normally in residence, although most of them were in the
streets that day, helping to restore order.

'Order!' I barked. 'They have no idea of what it is!'

'That is so, Excellency,' agreed Voss, while Joachim went
off without saying where he was going but asking my permission to leave the room. That, on the ground floor, was
plainly furnished as an office, but there were two comfortable easy chairs, one of which Joachim had placed for me
me before leaving. 'It has been said that unoccupied France
was at a point of revolution,' Voss continued, 'but the passing of reliable information has been difficult. There are
traitors on all sides.'

'Go on,' I said.

'Murdoch, of course, has arranged the trouble,' he told
me.

'You knew of him?'

'But yes, Excellency. I was first brought to Vichy two
months ago, and von Stroem asked for my services. Schlesser
in Paris released me. I soon learned that von Stroem suspected that Murdoch and Dell were causing this trouble,
and he hoped that as one who had worked for you for so
long I would be able to assist him. I confirmed the identity
of the agents.'

'Why did you not advise me?' I demanded. 'Information
should have been sent to me.'

'It was sent, Excellency,' Voss assured me. 'But as I heard nothing from you I knew that it was not being allowed to reach you. Baron von Stroem was extremely reluctant to bring you here.'

I could believe that; was there ever so despicable a hypocrite as von Stroem, or so contemptible a coward?

'I have been working in Vichy for some weeks,' went on Voss, 'and I can present you with a comprehensive picture of the situation, Excellency. I have not told von Stroem everything, I was obtuse, I made continued references to you until at last he was persuaded that only you could deal with Murdoch.'

'So,' I said, breathing heavily, 'that is why von Stroem came to me. You have done well.'

'Thank you, Excellency.' Even then Voss looked unintelligent, and I did not need to exercise my imagination a great deal to know how he had acted with von Stroem, who must have thought him the biggest idiot in Germany or France!

'Proceed with your report,' I ordered.

Vichy, as well as other large towns in unoccupied France, was in a state of smouldering rebellion. It had started early in the winter, when the diversion of food supplies to Germany had been felt first in those countries controlled by the Reich. In Berchtesgarten I knew it was believed that the French and the people of other nations blamed the British for the state of semi-starvation in which they existed, which was what was intended.

But they had *not* blamed the British.

Curse them, curse every man and woman and child among them! They nursed a hatred of the Reich, hatred which only the whip will cure. They had been treated too well; this was the result.

'This part of France was in particularly poor condition at the end of the winter,' continued Voss, 'and consequently it was perfect ground for Murdoch. He has nursed the spirit of rebellion carefully, and has it under his control. The food riots are less riots than organised looting, Excellency. Even our own warehouses have been raided, and food has been distributed free by People's Commissars.'

Again I thought that there was an odd expression in Voss's

145

eyes, and I was not wrong, for he continued: 'There is one remarkable thing.'

'Proceed,' I said.

'It is this, Excellency. Had Murdoch desired, Vichy, and perhaps all of unoccupied France, would have been in revolt two months ago. The people *wanted* it. But Murdoch, Fuller and Angell, they have prevented it from coming. It has puzzled me, Excellency.'

And I could well understand that! Murdoch had brought the country to a pitch of revolt but then refused to give the word which would have brought rebellion.

Why? I became obsessed by the question. Why had he held his hand? Most certainly, he had a reason which justified this in his mind.

22

More of Mondel

'There is some purpose behind their delay,' said Voss, 'and I have been doing everthing possible to find out what. I know in a measure how it is done. Through Fuller and Angell and others Murdoch has brought here many of the agents of the Free French Committee. They have promised more food and clothing if the local people will hold their hand for a time. By pillaging shops and stores throughout France—stores which were kept in readiness for our troops, these supplies have been found. While he keeps his promise, the people will obey him.'

I said: '*Ach,* it is the Free French. Murdoch is helping them, but only the French could have arranged this in France.'

'That is so,' said Voss.

'And perhaps that fine Free Frenchman, de Gaulle, imagines that he can name the appointed time,' I said harshly. 'I will see every town and city in France smashed beyond repair before it is allowed! It is not yet too late. Have the woman brought in. It may be possible,' I added very softly, 'to persuade her to talk.'

He eyed me with a faint smile on his lips.

'That will not surprise me, Excellency.'

For some minutes I was alone.

I thought of Dell, and the dreams I had had, of the wretches I had seen tormented, disfigured, deformed. I wondered what the realisation would be like, for I knew she would not talk freely.

The door opened to admit her.

She must have known something of what was ahead of her, but she walked without support and held her head high. There was in her eyes an expression which I always disliked—like the lash of a whip. Her short hair was dishevelled, and at her lips, especially the corners, there were angry red patches where the gag had been tied.

Voss, Joachim and a third man came behind her.

The third man's surname I do not know—Joachim called him Franz. He was short and stocky, and his mind was undeveloped, his sloping forehead and small eyes proved that. I did not doubt that he had attended many similar examinations.

I said: 'So, you have made another mistake, Fräulein.' It was wise, I thought, for me to be courteous on the surface; I had to hide my exultation. I did not wish her to suspect that I *wanted* to see her suffer: she needed to believe that I was interested only in making her talk, and that as soon as she had done so she would be free from threat of further pain.

'Mistake?' she asked and her voice was quite steady.

'You imagined that I would never go free again, that I did not see who you were,' I said, and I believe that she was genuinely startled. 'Fräulein, you underrate me, as you have always done. I was aware of the danger and the difficulties which my mission would bring, but I was quite confident of their outcome. I arranged for my assistant to come quickly after me—the result of which you know.'

'I know that you are a liar,' she said.

I clenched my hand, as Joachim said softly: 'Franz.'

The other man took out a rubber truncheon. I had suspected why he had kept his hand in his pocket all the time.

147

He struck her heavily across the buttocks where it hurt, but did no damage. She was jolted forward, her fine pose quite lost. But she kept her hands in front of her, although the skin on the knuckles glistened white.

'You will be wise to watch your words,' I told her. 'I have no desire to see you suffer, Fräulein, but you will understand that the cause of the Fatherland must come first, and I intend to know what you can tell me before you leave this room.'

'I shall tell you nothing,' she said.

The insolence of her!

Franz hit her on the side of the head; it is a painful blow but one which must be well-judged, or it will bring unconsciousness too early. She staggered to one side but Voss pushed her back again.

'You are forgetting where you are,' I said softly. 'Fräulein, I wish to know two things. What are your dealings with Mondel, and why have you delayed the outbreak of a rebellion which I have known for some time you could arrange when you chose?'

'If you know so much,' she said, 'how is it you know nothing of Mondel?'

'You are mistaken,' I said swiftly. 'You have to confirm my knowledge. I will have your story, Fräulein.'

She actually took a step towards me, although Joachim took her wrist, preventing her from coming too far. Franz took the other wrist, and I saw his thick fingers tighten. He began to twist her arm slowly from above the elbow. Only a man who had studied such methods thoroughly could have done that. The pain in the shoulder becomes excruciating.

I saw her bite her lips, but it did not stop her from saying:

'You know precisely nothing—you are a fraud, Baron von Horssell. You pick the bones others throw at you. You will learn nothing from me. Bruce will handle you—this will be one more debt to pay.'

Franz released her arm—it is not necessary to twist too long—and struck her on the side of the jaw. Her head jolted backwards, and she drew in a sharp breath. But I was impatient, for her manner suggested that she had come prepared to suffer, and that a long series of promptings would avail me little. I stood up from my chair and approached her. I stretched out my left arm, and I gripped her throat. I had to force myself not to squeeze too hard.

'You will talk, and talk now,' I said. 'If you refuse you will be stripped and beaten. There will not be an inch of skin left on your back. Have you . . .'

She jerked herself away from me! Her movement itself was not enough to make that possible, but she also lifted her hand, and she was carrying a needle or a pin, for the point stuck into me and involuntarily I released my grip. She did not try to get further away—Joachim and Franz prevented that—but she spoke swiftly, staring at me all the time. The pupils of her eyes were tiny; I did not realise why just then.

Her voice was low-pitched and harsh.

'You are all I thought you were and worse,' she said. 'You are lower than any animal. You have the mind of a cesspool and the blood of a snake.' It is difficult for me now to make her words appear as cutting as they did; scorn, contempt, hatred—all those and more were in them, and her voice.

'Yes, I know what you will do, or try to do. I have spent six months in Europe since I last saw you. I have seen the women you have finished with—you and the degenerates you fight for. I have seen them blinded, I've seen girls of sixteen and seventeen look like old women, I've seen them mutilated and deformed, lashed until the blood could flow no more, raddled with acid—I've *seen* them, victims of the Nazi beasts, there is no other word. *And* I've heard their stories. I talked with a convent child of fifteen, who had seen a Polish officer in hiding and would not say where. She was raped until she was unconscious, and when I saw her she had neither breasts nor fingers.'

This accursed woman made it sound much worse than it was as she spoke in a low harsh voice.

'I shall take revenge for them, through Bruce—on you and your servants. But you will never get the pleasure of seeing me maltreated.'

I swallowed hard as a thought went through my mind, that she had taken poison. I realised then that morphia and

149

other poisons will make the pupils of the eyes become pin points, as they did then.

Franz lifted his truncheon.

'Stop!' I ordered. 'Dell, what have you taken?'

She laughed at me.

She started on a low note, and then her voice went higher; it had a maniacal sound. Her eyes widened, and I saw the pinpoint-size pupils. I shouted at her to stop; Franz struck her several times, once breaking the skin near her chin. But she went on and on; it seemed that nothing would stop her short of deliberately making her unconscious.

Then she stopped and but for the men holding her she would have fallen heavily. They let her crumple onto the ground, where she lay in a huddled heap. Franz kicked her on the shin, but she showed no sign of feeling.

Would she die?

That was mostly what I asked myself. Would she die with the knowledge which she had in her mind? I lost sight then of personal issues, I was concerned only with keeping her alive so that I could force her to talk.

I snapped: 'Get her to bed. Find a doctor. Tell him the symptoms are of morphine poisoning by injection, but I cannot be sure it was not oral. Hurry!' I shouted, and Franz turned and rushed out of the room.

The woman's mouth was open a little.

I knelt beside her, and I saw just inside her mouth, tied by fine cord or string to a back tooth, a small rubber ball, with one side punctured. I knew she had carried that in her mouth so that it would not be detected, and that by biting on it she had released poison from inside.

She must have doubted her strength to withstand the methods of persuasion, and secreted the drug. But I did not believe she would kill herself. I believed she would perhaps be under the influence of the drug for some hours, possibly a day—but she would not kill herself unless it was certain she had no chance at all to escape.

I pulled the little rubber sachet away.

'She will not use that again,' I said to Joachim. 'When she comes round she will be more amenable.' I straightened up, admitting to myself that I was perplexed. It was as if

150

no matter what the circumstances Murdoch and Dell were never wholly in my power.

I was aware of a voice saying softly: 'Excellency!'

It was repeated three or four times before I looked at the speaker, and my eyes cleared to show me Voss. His vacant face was set in apologetic lines. I thought for a moment that the man was the fool he looked.

'What is it?' I rasped.

'Excellency,' said Voss. 'There is one good thing. I have heard rumours of Mondel's hiding place.'

∙ ∙ ∙ ∙ ∙

As abruptly as that the situation changed.

Mondel was the key to the problem. I knew so little of him and then only what I had heard from men who had deliberately lied to me. I only know that fixed in my mind above all other things was the need for finding this man, who according to reports was hidden somewhere near Vichy.

Murdoch did not know where.

I looked at Voss, who said hurriedly:'

'There has been so little time, Excellency, and I did not have the opportunity of telling you before.'

I drew a deep breath, and was hardly aware that Joachim had gone out of the room again.

'It is understood,' I said. 'Where is Mondel?'

'I cannot be sure,' said Voss. 'But you will know that in spite of the situation in France we have many agents, and their reports are constantly reaching Paris. There is a rumour that Mondel is in an old farmhouse ten miles from Vichy. The exact position is not known, but daily—hourly —possible places are being visited. I have arranged for word to be telephoned to me at *l'Hôtel Grande* immediately it is received.'

'Where did the information come from?' I demanded.

He took out his wallet.

He has the oddest way of acting, even with me. He bowed, and actually looked nervous as he presented me with the wallet, opened to show a number of letters and

151

reports in one section. I took them out, and I read three reports.

I realised then how thoroughly he—and Schlesser in Paris—had been working. They were far more acutely aware of the danger than I had been, and also knew the importance of Mondel. Consequently they had sent orders that all costs he was to be located. There was a letter from a man who had discovered Mondel's private secretary, on a country road, and had arranged for her to be questioned. She had been stubborn, but had finally said that he was in a farmhouse.

She had died before she had identified the place, the fools who had questioned her had been too zealous.

There was another. The editor of *Le Noir,* one of Mondel's papers circulating in Vichy and the surrounding district, had been suspected of knowing where to find his employer. He had been visited in his office, but he too had been obstinate, although he had also used the word 'farmhouse'. There the report ended, and I looked up at Voss.

'Did he also die?'

'No—no, Excellency,' said Voss awkwardly. 'But he collapsed—he is now in hospital. He will be questioned the moment he recovers.'

I grunted. 'Always it is too late.'

The third report, more guarded, said that Mondel's daughter had been seen coming into Vichy disguised as a farmer's housewife; a clumsy description, that. She had left Vichy the same night, but had eluded her pursuers.

'Daughter,' I said thoughtfully. 'So he has a daughter.'

'She is charming,' said Voss, grinning widely.

'I don't care if she is as ugly as a Gorgon!' I rasped. 'If she is seen again, she must be brought to me. But there is perhaps another way. Arrange for word to be sent about that I want a word with Mondel personally. Advertise, if you must—arrange it. I have a proposition for him but a meeting must be arranged. You understand?'

'It will be difficult, Excellency,' demurred Voss.

'Have it done,' I told him.

He did not argue again, but was at the door when it opened to admit Joachim. Joachim carried a tray with coffee, and I was glad to see that. But I was puzzled more by the letter which was also on the tray.

'Who is this from?' I demanded.

'It was delivered by hand, Excellency, to *l'Hôtel Grande*. I have a messenger there who agreed to bring all correspondence here—he will not be suspected. Shall I open it?'

'Yes,' I said, handing him the letter.

It was addressed to Herr Horst, and had been delivered by hand to the hotel. I had in mind the possibility of a gas balloon such as that in the letter Elsa had received, or I would have opened it myself. Joachim slit the envelope with a knife, and there was no surprise trick, so I took the letter and glanced at the signature. And then I stared at it, hardly believing it; but the flowing letters were easily read. The signature was—or purported to be—*that of Jules Mondel.*

23

I Receive an Offer

I have deliberately said 'or purported to be' because I was aware even as I read the signature that it might be false. I could see no reason at all why Mondel should write to me, but could readily understand why Murdoch might want to start me on a trial which he could follow.

The letter was short. I thought as I read it that it lacked the extravagant phraseology which one comes to expect of the French, but I had to allow for the fact that the writer was—or purported to be—a newspaperman; they are masters in expressing themselves without wasting words, and I have often considered that Governments might be wise to follow their example instead of using a welter of circumlocution.

I have not a copy of the letter, but can remember it word for word. I recall even that the fourth word was crossed out hastily in pencil.

Herr Horst, Sir:

I have reason for believing that you will be glad to meet me to discuss certain matters of which you are acquainted. I am not averse to such discussion but it must be understood that any talk must be free on both sides, and without coercion. Because of the possibilty of coercion I have taken the precaution of hiding myself, but I will arrange to meet you at a spot within easy reach of Vichy if you will undertake to be accompanied only by your personal servant and Fräulein Elsa.

Your answer should be inserted in the form of a personal advertisement containing only the words 'yes, yes' in this afternoon's edition—or this evening's edition—of Le Noir.

Jules Mondel

I read this twice, then folded it, and looked into Voss's eyes. Joachim had poured me out some coffee, and I was only too glad of it. I remember wondering how much remained of my false strength; I was surprised that it had lasted for so long, for I had lost all count of time.

'How is the woman Dell?' I asked.

'She is being attended,' said Voss. 'There was a doctor at hand, Excellency. He has committed himself to no opinion yet.'

I nodded. 'And the other matter?'

Voss, let me say again is a remarkable man. When he has good news or a report which he knows is worthy of approbation he is hesitant and apologetic. When his report is a poor one, or his news bad, his manner is firm and confident.

'I have given the matter consideration, Excellency, and I have not yet seen a way in which it can be done.'

'Arrange for the insertion of a personal advertisement in the next edition of *Le Noir*,' I told him. 'It will say "yes, yes" and nothing more—the word "yes" twice, and with a comma in between. You understand?'

He clicked his heels. 'At once, Excellency.'

I was in a mood of tempered optimism, for thinking of the letter I could come only to the conclusion that it was from Mondel.

But I did not think it was as innocent as it sounded.

The fool, I thought! Doubtless he had heard that I was in the vicinity and would be replacing von Stroem. He had contrived to outwit von Stroem, and now wished to outwit me; it would suit the Frenchman well to have me killed, or incapacitated.

That was the obvious conclusion.

I felt the shooting pains in my leg again, and turned to Joachim.

'What time was I brought from the hotel?'

'A little over an hour ago, Excellency.'

I brooded for some minutes, and then Voss returned, nervous and hesitant. The advertisement had been telephoned and would be inserted in the edition then going to press —it would be on the streets within an hour. The doctor had now finished his examination: the woman Dell was suffering from morphine poisoning but not to a fatal degree. She would be unconscious for about twenty-four hours. The doctor would administer injections to endeavour to bring consciousness earlier, and the patient was to be kept in bed.

So she had not killed herself: I had been right on that calculation. Another factor then had to be considered—the possibility that Murdoch would try to get her back.

I said to Joachim: 'Is there a chair?'

'It is outside.' He went out, returning with a chair and a stick which, if it was not my original, was an exact replica. I was more comfortable when I was settled in the chair with my leg stretched in front of me, but far from easy in my mind. Mondel's letter had stipulated a 'personal' servant and Elsa.

I did not waste time in asking myself why he had mentioned Elsa. My concern was to find her, if that were possible. I had decided that I would go to this meeting place, and that I should be accompanied only by Joachim and one other—accompanied, that was, as far as Mondel would be able to see. I would stipulate that the meeting took place after dark.

I wanted the *person* of Mondel.

A bell rang somewhere outside, and Joachim went to answer it. I was not perturbed, for I was sure that they had brought me to a sanctuary where I need not fear inter-

155

ruption. For the first time I let myself see the truth: that when I had arranged for the capitulation of Belgium and of Holland, of Denmark and of Norway, I had been actually in a much weaker position that I was here in Vichy, where at least every man in five could be relied on.

Joachim returned, with another letter.

This time I was less careful, for I opened the envelope myself. It was a foolish thing to do, perhaps, but I recognised the writing, and I was quite sure there was no danger. *Elsa* had written to me at *l'Hôtel Grande*!

      *   *   *   *   *

For a moment I thought that Elsa had contrived to get free, and that prompted me to tear open the envelope, although Joachim's hand stretched out in mute protest. I drew out a single sheet of notepaper headed *l'Hôtel Berliner,* and I saw Elsa's back-sloping writing, with the heavy downstrokes.

Excellency,
*   I am writing this under compulsion. I am told that Murdoch is prepared to allow me to go free in exchange for Mary Dell. I need not assure you, Excellency, that I submit myself to your decision and am now as always only at the service to the Reich.*

That was all—an excellent letter. I had no doubt that she had written it herself, and not at dictation. It offered me a solution to my most urgent problem—that of finding Elsa; but I was reluctant to strike any bargain with Murdoch.

Could I contrive a way of making it seem to Murdoch that I would agree to the exchange, but retain Dell?

'Excellency'—Joachim had taken the envelope from me, and was now holding a second slip of paper in his hand—a smaller one, on which were typewritten words. 'This also was inside.'

I took it, half expecting what I found.

This letter was not started formally, and there was no signature. It merely said that if I agreed to the exchange Mary Dell was to be brought to *l'Hôtel Berliner*, alive at dusk that evening. Half an hour later, Elsa would be freed. I was left with the choice of accepting that ultimatum, and risking the possibility that Elsa would not be allowed to leave.

An odd thing is that I knew Murdoch would honour his pledge.

Had I imposed similar conditions I would not have carried out my undertaking. It is nonsense to talk of 'honour' in war and in such negotiations. There is no time or place for 'honour' as it is generally known. But Murdoch would not make a promise without keeping it.

I would not have agreed for anyone but Elsa. Even had Brunning been at my side I would have needed Elsa. Can anyone without such an infirmity as mine understand how much I depended on her? Elsa could think with me, sometimes even for me. Helpless as I was again, I needed her opinion; *in fact I was useless without her*.

That was not a palatable fact, and it was the first time that I had realised or admitted it. My thoughts were not pleasant. I did not want Mary Dell to go free.

Suddenly an idea flashed into my mind.

'Joachim—bring the doctor!' I ordered.

Voss had all the time been standing in the background, and he did not now ask questions, although he must have wondered what could be in the letters which I had received. It occurred to me that Murdoch must have assumed that some kind of arrangements had been made for the forwarding of my letters. It would be wise to move from this house without losing time. I told Voss of that decision.

He shifted his ungainly feet.

'I took leave to anticipate that possibility, Excellency, and have arranged a second house to which you can go under cover of darkness. I have only to telephone the final arrangements.'

'Good! Telephone at once,' I said.

He left the room a moment ahead of the doctor, a short, plump, red-faced man with a small pointed beard—a positive caricature of a Frenchman. I did not need to be told that he was with the Reich; Joachim and Voss would not have employed a man who could not be wholly trusted.

He bowed, spreading his hands in front of him palms downward.

'I am honoured, Excellency, to meet you.'

'You can do more,' I said. 'You can serve me.'

'I am waiting for that privilege, Excellency.'

'Good. Is there a drug which can be administered to the patient and which will prove fatal but not for some hours—a matter, say of three or four hours after its administration?'

He peered at me uncertainly; I heard Joachim draw in a sharp breath.

'It—it *could* be done, Excellency. It would be best in the form of a pill of morphia, containing a fatal dose. There are such pills which do not dissolve in the stomach for some hours—the exact time cannot be calculated, but a minimum of two hours can be guaranteed.'

'Have you such a pill?'

'I can prepare one, Excellency.'

'Do so. And prepare the patient for moving at dusk. There is one other thing—will it appear that she had died from the dose which was self-administered?'

'It would be difficult to decide one way or the other, Excellency, the symptoms would be exactly the same. Delayed death due to morphia is not unknown.'

His second piece of information not only confirmed the first, but put the finishing touch to a plan which had been hastily conceived and yet could not have been more thoroughly executed. Mary Dell would die as I meant her to die. But she would be alive when she reached Murdoch, and he would see her dying.

The mental torment Murdoch would suffer would be greater than physical torture. I would kill the one and take revenge on the other, but Murdoch would never be sure that I had killed her. *He would always consider it possible that a plan which he himself had evolved—that of keeping the drug in her mouth—had been the instrument of her death!*

The doctor went off to make his preparations, and I told Joachim what had been decided. He too was confident that if Dell reached Murdoch alive, Elsa would be released. I knew that without Dell, Murdoch would feel as lost as I did without Elsa, if for a different reason. The mental anxiety and the shock of losing her would do much to undermine his strength.

I wished that I could see von Stroem at that time, although I did not care much what happened to the man. I wanted only to have more news of the meeting which the Führer had ordered to be arranged, and I believed von Stroem to be in a state of mind in which he would tell me the truth.

Again I asked myself why Murdoch had persuaded the French people to be patient. I think I was nearer the truth than I had been before, and nearer than I was until the actual revelation burst upon me. In the next hour I arranged for Voss to report on the situation in Vichy and the surrounding countryside, and what I discovered was in a measure reassuring. Truly things were not as bad as I had feared. For a long time, troops had filtered through into unoccupied France, ready to quell just such a rising as seemed imminent. The troops were not mechanised, but they had small machine-guns. In a fifty-mile radius, Voss was able to assure me, there were ten thousand such troops. They were not congregated in any particular area—in Vichy itself there were perhaps two thousand—but many of them were supposedly refugees from Alsace; their accent was less noticeable because of that.

I asked: 'Voss, if this is the case, why has Murdoch been allowed to reach his present ascendancy?'

Voss shifted and stuttered.

'I—I cannot b-be sure, Excellency. My opinion—the opinion which I have formed to—to the best of my— my . . .'

'Yes, yes!' I snapped at him. 'Your opinion—what is it?'

'This, Excellency,' he said more steadily. 'Murdoch and the other British and Free French agents have gradually created the spirit of revolt among the people, yet the people do not wish to fight in the streets if it can be avoided, and do not wish to be bombed. That is reasonable. They prefer a peaceful settlement of their problems of getting more good food and work. They will take over the Government and the city if they can be sure it can be done quickly, but at the backs of their minds there is always thought of the

159

Luftwaffe, and of the tanks. Mondel, through his papers, has always advocated prudence. And that is why he has such a grip on the people. He has agitated against the Petain Government, now discredited throughout the country. You have perhaps been told that Mondel believes he will become the new President?'

'von Stroem voiced the thought, yes.'

'Mondel, then, has been sympathetic towards Murdoch because Murdoch had released food and other things,' went on Voss. 'But Mondel is for *France*, not for the Allies. If Mondel is convinced that under his leadership conditions will be better, he will discourage fighting. For that reason the meeting with the Führer—God save him!—was arranged. When Mondel disappeared it was believed that Murdoch had taken him, that was why von Stroem appealed to you. Now it transpires that Mondel disappeared of his own accord. He holds the balance between Murdoch and us, Excellency. If you meet him, you can persuade him . . .' He hesitated for a moment, and then continued: 'I am glad you inserted the advertisement but I implore you to accept the terms of the Frenchman's offer to the letter. Go only with the Fräulein and one other.'

He regarded me frankly, while I stared at him, silent for a moment and then demanding in a low voice

'Your advice may be well intended, Voss, but—*how do you know what terms Mondel offered?*'

24

Exchange of Prisoners

Only I had read Mondel's letter.

That remark, of course, needs qualifying; only I had read Mondel's words after they had reached me, but I could not be sure whether the message had been intercepted on the way. But I could not believe that Voss would have opened the letter and then resealed it.

Could he have read it upside-down while it was in my hand?

I stared at him coldly, and his manner was assured, as it is always when he is inwardly perturbed.

'I knew that such a proposition was considered, Excellency. It was once put to von Stroem. He accepted, but took a strong force of men with him. The force was wiped out in the hills, and von Stroem was fortunate to escape with his life. That is why I dare to advise you, and why I deduced that when you inserted an advertisement in one of Mondel's papers it was a similar reply to one made by von Stroem.'

I considered the answer in all its aspects, and finally I decided that it was probably genuine. I still disliked the thought of going to Mondel, wherever he arranged a meeting, with only Joachim and Elsa. Yet I did not say so to Voss; it is rarely wise to let others know what is in one's mind.

I nodded, and dismissed the subject by saying:

'First I will receive Mondel's next letter. It must come quickly. The important meeting with the Führer is for the day after tomorrow.'

'At two o'clock, Excellency.'

'Murdoch also knew the time,' I rasped. 'Murdoch . . .' I stopped, and then I began to smile, for looking up from the window I saw that dusk was falling. Just then Joachim came in, the doctor just behind him. Joachim had obtained another wheel chair. I could see it outside with Mary Dell sitting in it. She was pale and unconscious, and her eyes were closed, with dark rings about them.

'The tablet is ready, Excellency,' said the doctor.

'I will administer it myself,' I said.

I wheeled my chair myself to the door, and turned it so that my left hand was nearest the Englishwoman. She was breathing faintly, her lips slightly parted. I took the pill, a large one, from the doctor's hand. He opened her mouth very simply by pinching her nose and pulling her head back, so that her mouth was wide and I could see to the back of her throat. I inserted the tablet and as I pushed it down her gullet she gulped.

I said sharply: 'Can we be sure it will go down?'

'I have arranged that, Excellency,' said the doctor. 'If you will permit me ...'

He had a long, pliable object with him which looked to be of steel, with a small and soft rubber ball at one end. I watched him force the tablet past the larynx, and saw the muscles of Mary Dell's throat working as she swallowed.

The tablet disappeared.

I watched her for perhaps five minutes before her throat muscles stopped working and she was again in a state of complete stupor.

I nodded, and said, 'Take her to *l'Hôtel Berliner*, Joachim, and come back here at once.'

Without waiting for his reply I wheeled my chair back into the room. I cannot explain what followed, and I shall never try to. But I can say that I stared bleakly towards the closed door with a strange heaviness within me—a heaviness of depression when there should have been elation.

What *are* the forces which move in a man?

My depression did not last, but neither did it lift entirely. I worked with a feverish application which was not familiar, although it was not long before I put thought of Mary Dell out of my mind. I must record that for the first quarter of an hour that was extremely difficult. I could see her so clearly in my mind's eye—the Dell of the photograph which I had shown von Stroem.

Not until thought of her was out of my mind did I lose the weight of depression. But I could not rest, and I told myself that this restlessness was due to anxiety for Elsa, fear that Murdoch would not carry out his promise.

Voss and Joachim worked with me.

We went through the records and the reports which Voss had prepared for von Stroem. The more important facts he had copied on thin paper which he carried with him, and I was able to read them and to get the facts firmly in my mind. Perhaps of greatest importance was the number and the position of German troops in the vicinity. His estimate of ten thousand was low; there were nearer eleven thousand. Arms and ammunition for them were in a hundred places throughout the district. Hay-lofts, old barns, disused and partly demolished houses, cellars—yes, and sometimes in pits dug deep into the ground. The organisation had been excellent, and I asked who had arranged it.

'von Stroem,' answered Voss.

'He was in a different mood from what he has been of late,' I remarked. 'How long ago was this, Voss?'

'Some seven months, Excellency, soon after your return from England. In the early days of the occupation of France when it was easier to do what we wished than it is now. von Stroem always considered the possibility of a rising, and prepared against it.'

I would have done the same myself, and Voss knew it. I could not understand how it had happened that von Stroem had allowed himself to deteriorate so much—and yet I should have known.

For next came the sabotage reports.

They were positively startling. It is not perhaps generally known that a great deal of French ammunition and guns were despatched from unoccupied France to other parts of the country soon after the conquest of France, and a regular flow of such goods was afterwards maintained; France was also the repair-shop of the Reich.

Armament trains had been destroyed frequently; bridges were blown up, thus causing delay after delay. Petrol, that most precious of all commodities, had been fired not once but a hundred times. The small allowance made to Vichy must have been four-fifths destroyed before it could be used, and to maintain essential services other fuel was imported from Greater Germany.

Power stations were frequently damaged, particularly in the industrial areas. I had known some of this, but the degree was appalling. Yet as I read, and was told, of these continual outrages I was in a detached frame of mind, for I knew that I had prepared similar things myself. Murdoch had worked as if he had made a complete study of my own methods.

The estimate which Voss made of the number of people in the Vichy district prepared to work for Murdoch—or perhaps it would be best to say for Free France—was one in every twenty of the population, male and female. These were embittered and unalienable opponents of Germany, the type who should have been executed long ago. There had been some purges, but these had stopped three months before. It grew more and more obvious that Murdoch had contrived to obtain a hypnotic influence over von Stroem— or perhaps it would be truer to admit that when von Stroem made his various arrangements for purges and executions, Murdoch found a way of blocking them. Men taken as suspects for certain sabotage were 'proved' to have been elsewhere, and I quickly saw the difficulty of von Stroem's position. Executions out of hand would have been dangerous, and executions on the evidence were impossible.

In addition to the lists of German troops available, there were lists of known revolutionaries, but these were never in the same place for long, and usually the quarters they decided to occupy were so well guarded that only by a considerable display of force could they be broken.

von Stroem had not wanted to use that force, for it would have been a confession of failure. But I was in a different situation altogether; I had to put right the mistakes of von Stroem, and could use force with impunity.

I was glad, however, that I had not sent an urgent message to Berchtesgarten for a considerable movement of troops and aeroplanes. The new figures showed the situation in a truer perspective, and with the men at my command I could get Vichy under control within forty-eight hours.

Throughout all the reports and statements the figure of Mondel loomed large, and when I had finished I knew that von Stroem was right; Mondel *must* be won over to the side of the Reich.

I gathered from what I read that the newspaperman was a strong character. Voss actually likened him to Reynaud, and although I have nothing but detestation for that man I will admit that he was the strongest French politician I have known, with the possible exception of Herriot and Blum. I am talking, of course, of the past decade, not of the previous Great War.

Out of the facts and figures, the occasional words from Voss and from Joachim, there emerged a clear picture of Mondel, and I realised above all things that he was not a man who could be intimidated. It would be wise for the time being to placate him, to give him full assurance that the Reich would not interfere with the part of France which remained 'independent' if he took the Presidency.

And he would need convincing of the Reich's sincerity.

I turned abruptly to Voss.

'Who first suggested Mondel's meeting with the Führer?'

'Mondel himself, Excellency.'

'To von Stroem?'

'Yes, Excellency.'

'And von Stroem went to Berchtesgarten to arrange it. Has it occured to you, Voss, that the Leader will find it advisable in the event of the meeting to placate Mondel?'

Voss shuffled his feet.

'In my opinion, yes, Excellency, and I believe that von Stroem realised that. I believe that the meeting will be in a cordial atmosphere. It has been said that the Führer—God be with him!—is anxious to make concessions to France in order to rid himself of the possibility of an uprising.'

'Yes,' I agreed. 'That will be necessary. And for the first time I realise why this interview cannot be faked. von Stroem was quite right when he said that Mondel must be saved from falling into Murdoch's hands.' I fell silent, and Voss continued to shuffle and to sniff until I barked at him to stop, or to speak if he had something on his mind.

'It is this, Excellency,' he said, growing more confident; so what he had to say was distasteful. 'I had the temerity to advise on your method of approach to Mondel because I had these considerations in mind.'

I said sharply: 'I will accept Mondel's conditions. I shall not endeavour to evade them. But there must be a force at hand strong enough to support me in the event of trickery on Mondel's part, or interruption from Murdoch. Have that made clear to Mondel if you are able to get a message to him.'

'He will make it possible when he reads the advertisement,' said Voss.

By the clock I took an hour and a half to go through the papers, and the sudden cessation of concentration made me deflated. But Joachim had prepared coffee, and drinking it,

I recalled Mary Dell for the first time, and also that Elsa should by now have arrived. I started up in my chair, and it must have been some sixth sense which had brought her to my mind then, for the telephone rang suddenly, and Voss answered it.

I heard his voice rise a little in excitement.

'It is the Fräulein, Excellency! She is at *l'Hôtel Grande*. And Excellency—von Stroem has also been released!'

25

I Meet Mondel

I do not think that I shall ever be able to understand Murdoch. Who would have dreamed that the man would not only carry out his obligation, but go further and send von Stroem back as well as Elsa? I had written von Stroem off as lost, and not a great loss either.

There is one possible explanation; Murdoch was so pleased to see his woman back that in a moment of emotional generosity he gave thanks with the person of von Stroem.

Thanks—for a woman who was dying!

I grow weary of saying that I cannot explain it. I have tried a thousand times in the past year to understand, but I cannot. It was almost as if I wished that I had not thrust that fatal tablet into Mary Dell's mouth. But that was madness! I should make it clear that these attempts to understand and to explain have taken place since those days in Vichy. At the time I was aware only that I did not get the anticipated pleasure out of my triumph. I told myself that I was too concerned with the other problems to savour it, but normally I have never been happier than when facing a task which most would have called impossible.

I forced myself to speak.

'Have them instructed to go to the alternative rendezvous, Voss. We shall go there at once.'

'Yes, Excellency.' He spoke into the telephone for a

166

moment. Joachim meanwhile had found one of my great-coats, with a large fur collar—I am susceptible to cold about the neck—and helped me into it. Less then twenty minutes afterwards I reached the secondary rendezvous. I could not see what it was like outside, but inside it was clearly a house which had once belonged to a wealthy family; the furnishing was luxurious and expensive, the degree of comfort was considerable.

There was a study on the ground floor.

I was wheeled towards it, and I saw the door open. Elsa stood in front of me.

Her eyes were shining, lovely amber eyes which I had not thought to see again. Her lips were open wide to show her fine white teeth, and the tip of her tongue glistened. Had I not known it I would have refused to believe that she had just been reprieved from a sentence of death.

I smiled at her and my depression eased; it was so good to see her.

'And so, Elsa, you are back!'

'I am glad, Excellency.' She was formal because von Stroem was standing in the background. I could imagine his feelings, for after his display at the hotel he would know that he had no power or authority left—automatically I assumed it. 'I am glad, Excellency,' she repeated, 'that you considered me of such value to the Reich that you made such a sacrifice.'

'Sacrifice?' I grunted.

'In freeing Mary Dell,' she said.

I wondered what she would think when she learned the truth. I wondered whether I should delay telling her, and that was surprising, for I might have been expected to be full of it. However, I saw no object in delay.

'Had it been necessary I would have made the ex-change.'

She stared, and von Stroem looked towards me as if startled.

'Had it been *necessary*?' echoed Elsa. 'I am at a loss, Ex-cellency. The Dell woman was released. I saw her.'

I barked: 'By now she will be dead.'

I do not think that Elsa believed me. I saw von Stroem step forward suddenly, his face glowing. The wound in his cheek had been well-dressed, and the inflammation there as well as at his eye and lip was considerably reduced.

'Dead, von Horssell?' he demanded.

I looked at him coldly.

'I arranged it,' I declared. 'She received another dose of the drug which she was clever enough to use to save herself from injury.' I took pleasure in describing exactly what had happened, and in praising the ingenuity of the doctor. Elsa's smile disappeared—that is all I can say. It disappeared; there was no gladness in her.

But I had never seen von Stroem forget himself so much as he did then.

'You got her,' he nearly shouted. 'You've killed her, you've smashed Murdoch! Nothing could be better, Excellency.'

'Murdoch remains,' I said coldly. 'Have the goodness to control yourself.'

In front of Voss and Joachim that was a rebuke which, two days before, would have called for the strongest protest from von Stroem, but when only he, Elsa and myself were in the study he made no comment. His spirit was quite gone, although I could well understand that it had been momentarily revived when he had learned of the devastating blow that had fallen on Murdoch and Dell.

I was not prepared to tell von Stroem exactly what I was planning. I gave him instead a brief resumé of the least important points, then requested him to try to contact with Schlesser in Paris. Brunning should be there by now. I had given very little thought to Brunning since he had started for Paris.

When the door had closed, Elsa said slowly:

'And so we are winning, Ludvic.'

'The personal matters are not important,' I reminded her. 'The greater issues remain to be settled. von Stroem will not be long, and it is necessary to make some pretence at consulting with him for the time being. You are attentive?'

'I am waiting,' she replied.

I gave her the gist of what had happened, and from time to time she nodded her approval. I was feeling better. The thought of forthcoming action and the meeting with Mondel, which I had taken for granted, were thrusting

168

other thoughts from my mind. I finished by suggesting that Mondel's letter might be intended as a trap.

She shook her head decisively.

'He wishes to consult with you,' she said. 'He wanted to see von Stroem but the fool failed in the conditions. He has been telling me of it. Mondel will not set a trap. The only other possibility of deceit is Murdoch.'

'That is so.'

'And if Murdoch had wanted he could have killed you from the start,' she said. 'He would not need to go to the trouble of luring you anywhere. No, Ludvic—this is an approach from Mondel.'

'It is also my opinion,' I said.

'There is one danger,' continued Elsa, taking a cigarette from a handbag which I did not recognise.

'That is not your bag,' I interrupted. 'I brought it away.'

'Thank you,' she said. 'It is one of Mary Dell's. Murdoch gave it to me, as I was without one—it contains everything I need.' She spoke hurriedly and quickly, and continued at once with her 'one danger' theme.

'If Murdoch wants Mondel badly, and he certainly does, he will follow you in the hope of seeing the Frenchman at the same time, or at least of negotiating with him after your interview. The danger is that of being followed.'

'It will be settled,' I said, 'when we hear from Mondel.'

I was looking at the bag. It was a small one, of soft navy blue leather. I kept looking at it although my mind was on Mondel and the coming interview. Yet I had to ask questions, had to do something more than plan and scheme ahead.

'You saw Murdoch?' I asked.

'Yes.' I had an impression that she did not wish to discuss it. 'He talked, as he always does. He is a fool in more ways than one, Excellency.' I noticed the return to formality, and wondered what caused it. 'Angell and Fuller were also present. I had the impression that without Mondel's support, they cannot succeed in what they are attempting. I think that is why they have delayed any action. If they moved without Mondel's support, the townsfolk might be in agreement, the peasants would not. That is reasonable.'

'It is,' I conceded.

'Murdoch appeared quite confident of success.' She shrugged, and then she said a surprising thing: 'It is a pity he was born in the wrong country, Excellency.'

I stared at her. 'You think that?'

'He is worth a hundred Brunnings,' she said abruptly.

I thought then—and for the first time since I had been able to get away and to capture Dell—of my weakness of the previous night, and my jealousy of Brunning. Jealousy it was, and by then I was prepared to acknowledge it. I was aware then she had little more than contempt for Brunning, and she had put into words an impression which I have had myself.

Had Murdoch been a German he would have been a great man, one with whom I would have been proud to work. I thrust the thought aside.

Soon afterwards there came a message from Mondel. It was clear that someone in Vichy had telephoned him about the advertisement, and that the someone had arranged for a letter to be sent to *l'Hôtel Grande*. From there, thanks to Voss and Joachim, it was brought quickly to me.

It was wholly satisfactory.

It told me precisely where to meet Mondel on the following day, at two o'clock, precisely twenty-four hours before the Leader was due to meet him. It described the meeting-place in detail, and it repeated its condition; only Elsa and Joachim were to be with me.

I thought of what I had told Voss.

I wanted more support in case it should prove a trick, yet I could see no way of passing on my conditions to Mondel. I cursed the Frenchman for his cunning; I had to wait for him.

Elsa understood my doubts.

'I believe you can trust him,' she declared. 'It is going to be a case of necessity, Baron. If he believes that you are going to try to take him prisoner it may prove fatal.'

'Fatal!' I shouted. 'Will it not be fatal if I am taken a prisoner. Have you forgotten yourself so much in your admiration for Murdoch that you have lost sight of the vital importance of what we are doing? Can you not understand that if France should revolt under the leadership of a man such as Mondel may prove, it could be the death blow at the Third Reich? Is your head so thick that you cannot perceive the dangers of a revolution throughout the largest country dominated by the Nazi rule? Have you failed to perceive the fact that a million men would be needed to bring the country to a state of order if once the yoke slips from the necks of the French bastards? We stand or fall by the successful control of the countries we conquer— *we stand or fall*!' I shouted at her, suddenly beside myself and shaking my left hand at her, even trying to rise in my chair. 'Am I to submit myself to the mercy of a man who may be in league with Murdoch and with de Gaulle? Am I...'

My throat grew so constricted that the words were beginning to choke me. I knew that if I went on I was liable to collapse and to prostration. I shivered from head to foot, and yet my very anger emphasised my uselessness without her.

She could have taken a sweet revenge.

Revenge for my shouting at her, for my loss of temper. For the years which I had compelled her to devote to me. For the wasted womanhood, as some might say, in which she had given herself freely and frequently to enemies of the Reich, that in her warmth and with her alluring voice in their ear they might forget their mission. Once she had tried to break Murdoch's love for Dell, and had failed; I cannot remember any other time she had failed with a man.

She could have taken refuge, I say, and have left me. I could not have stopped her. She could have shouted back. I wondered in the split-second in which I had to think what she would do, and also I wondered what had reduced me to a state of frenzy.

She said, as if I had not interrupted: 'And so we must trust Mondel, Ludvic. You are agreeable?'

I felt the muscles of my neck contracting, and the heat in my body subsiding until I became icy cold. But I was grateful. She would never desert me. I think she knew what was driving me—that wherever I looked I could see Mary Dell's eyes.

'It is so,' I grunted. 'We will trust Mondel.'

I will not spend a great deal of time or space in recording the events of the next twenty hours, to the time of my meeting with Jules Mondel. A brief summary will suffice.

Brunning returned safely from Schlesser with the reports and papers which served only to confirm that I had heard from Voss. The only other news he brought was that the Leader was in Paris, and proposed to travel by train for the meeting with Mondel; the fact that the Leader was travelling was not generally known. Schlesser, it appeared, had information that a great deal was expected of the meeting in Vichy.

von Stroem had said at Berchtesgarten that all the arrangements were completed. I would have said the same.

I talked to Voss and Brunning. They were to take command of a hundred men each, and to go within ten miles of my meeting place with Mondel, throwing a cordon about it. Unless I returned safely they would close in. In the event of the need for such action, they had many more men in support.

There were no reports of further rioting, although the area cordoned off that morning remained in the hands of the 'rioters'. I took the opportunity of conferring with the Chief of Police, who confirmed that von Stroem had told him not to do anything which would precipitate a general rising. I had to acknowledge von Stroem's perspicacity about that.

I heard nothing about Mary Dell.

Inquiries were made through Joachim and Voss, but all that transpired was that a specialist had been summoned to l'Hôtel Berliner soon after the woman had been returned, even before Elsa had been freed. I knew that Murdoch had trusted me to do to his woman what he had done to mine.

At last, it was time to start for the meeting with Mondel. Soon after one o'clock a special car, driven by Joachim, was brought to the house on the outskirts of Vichy. No suspicious characters had loitered near, and the house had been surrounded by the Gestapo: my whereabouts was not suspected.

Elsa sat beside me.

We might have been at the beginning of our quest, not near the end of it.

von Stroem had wanted to come, and I had refused adamantly. He had shouted, ordered, cursed; he had pleaded and begged; but I had refused. He wanted to wrest the final triumph from me; I did not propose to take the slightest risk of that. I passed through the countryside and past the people working in the fields, towards the hills, finally towards the narrow stone bridge over a small stream where I was to meet Mondel's emissary. I did not know who it would be; she would address me by name and that would identify her. Yes, a woman—so much I had been told. The only woman in sight when we reached the bridge was a girl beating clothes on the stones washed by the stream. Half-a-mile away I could see smoke rising from the chimney of a cottage; she had come from there. But as she saw the car she rose laboriously from her knees, limping as though they hurt her. She climbed to the bridge, and approached me: I knew she was coming to beg. I even decided that it might be wise to dispense *largesse* when she opened the door and said:

'The Baron von Horssell?'

The washerwoman, Mondel's emissary?

I was soon convinced, however.

There was no road to the lonely farmhouse which looked like a cottage, but the car could be driven to within a hundred yards of it. A copse of beech hid it from one side, and a stone path led through them to the house itself.

There was a folding chair, tied to the carrier of the car. Joachim unfastened it, and I sat down. A queer sight that must have been, the Baron Ludvic von Horssell, Elsa—dressed in rich furs—and Joachim pushing the chair over the uneven stones, tight-lipped because he knew that each lurch caused me pain.

The girl, whom I judged to be Mondel's daughter, led the way. She was thin, but a pretty thing. I watched her picking her way along the stones, and indeed the sound of the footsteps on stone walls was all I heard until the murmur of men's voices reached me, and I saw the two men, one with his back to me, the other facing me.

The latter was Mondel.

I had, of course, seen his photograph. He is a man of middle-age, grey-haired, and florid of skin. His eyes are peculiar; they are large but hooded, with the lids loose like those of a great bird. He is clean-shaven and fleshy, although none could call him fat. He was taller and bigger than I expected as he looked over the shoulder of the man in front of him. But despite the fact that I was meeting Mondel, I had eyes only for the second man.

It was von Stroem.

26

The Cordon Moves In

I wanted to hurry, but I knew that Joachim could push no faster on that uneven path. Mondel was looking towards me, and his companion must have known who was coming, but von Stroem continued to talk in a low-pitched voice.

He stopped at last, and turned.

I expected to find him haggard and despairing, but apparently the finding of Mondel had given fresh spirit, for he had the impertinence to bow, and to speak as he had done in the study of my home.

'Good afternoon, Excellency. I trust the journey has not proved too much for you.'

I ignored him completely, regarding Mondel.

'M'sieu Jules Mondel?' I asked, and he bowed, distantly I thought. He was dressed in a soiled blue shirt, a beret, and a pair of shabby grey trousers; a similar dress is worn by every peasant and smallholder in France. But he had made no attempt to disguise his face.

'The Baron von Horssell,' he said. 'I am glad to meet you. I am afraid my hospitality is limited, but we will talk inside if you have no objection.'

'None,' I said. 'But I would like a word with Baron von Stroem in private.'

'That can be arranged,' said Mondel mildly.

Inside, the farmhouse was furnished well and cleanly. I have since learned that it was one of many such places which Mondel, one of the richest men in France, had bought and repaired and decorated for quiet weekends. He visited them not with his mistress, but with his wife—who had died in England where she had gone for safety—and his daughter, who now removed her wet apron and went upstairs.

Mondel followed her, and I eyed von Stroem.

His eyes were shifty, but he could not keep them averted all the time. I let the silence continue for some seconds before I said heavily:

'Is this the way you carry out instructions, von Stroem?'

He licked his lips, but made an effort to show authority.

'I have yet to learn that you can instruct me.'

'It is time you learned precisely what I am doing,' I told him. I felt quite cool and detached, and there was no fear of me losing my temper. 'I have taken the opportunity of writing a full and comprehensive report of everything I have discovered, and I have sent it by special courier to Berchtesgarten. You understand what that means?'

He drew back a pace, his hands clenched.

'You swine! You have betrayed . . .'

'It is enough!' I snapped. 'You may go. When I return to Vichy there will be a countrywide search for you, and if you are found *alive*,' I added very softly, 'it will be the occasion of an inquiry much more severe than that which you instituted for the Chief of Police in Vienna.'

Joachim had a gun in his hand, but I did not think he would need to use it. For some seconds von Stroem glared at me, with his ugly, bloodshot eyes; then he turned and went out of the room.

'That was well done,' said Elsa.

I raised my voice: 'M'sieu Mondel, I am at your service.'

He had changed, and was dressed in a good-fitting lounge suit when he returned to the main room. He was smoking a cigar, asked whether I objected, and when I shook my head he said quietly enough:

'Now, Excellency. There is no purpose in wasted words. I have a considerable power in France, and I think that I can persuade the country to revolt—which is already in embryo—if that is the only way of achieving justice.'

That was frankness beyond doubt! Despite his promise

175

of such talk I had not expected anything like such a degree of forthrightness. This man was negotiating with me, the representative of the victor nation, a long time after the signing of an Armistice, yet dared to talk thus.

It confirmed what I had been discovering throughout the past two days. Many French people were ready for revolution if it should prove the only way to settle their differences with both the Vichy Government and the Reich. But was the whole of the country prepared for rebellion?

Vichy was: how many other cities, how many villages and small towns? It must be remembered that the threat of Italian action on the other frontiers had been removed, and that at the time the people of France were fully aware of the other difficulties with which the Reich was faced.

'M'sieu Mondel,' I said, 'you suggest making terms, but such terms could only be operative if we assume your power to instigate rebellion. As you say, it is wise to talk frankly. However, I need not remind you that by such talk you are breaking the clauses of the Armistice, but we are practical men . . .'

'I am glad you realise that,' said Mondel, and his smooth and courteous voice told me that here was a deadly man with great strength of intellect and a firm grasp of practical considerations. The would-be President of a new and really independent France was talking to me in the low-ceilinged room of a hovel!

'Because,' he continued, 'I know of no single clause of the Armistice which Petain signed that you have not broken, Herr Baron. I did not expect otherwise.'

I wondered why he considered that we would keep any agreement made now with a subject nation; but men are like that. Even the cleverest are credulous. Petain, Badouin, Laval and a dozen others had failed to get what they wanted, but Mondel possessed a vanity which persuaded him he could succeed. Vanity was his weakness; each man has one.

'Nothing was broken which was not necessary for the good of your country and people,' I told him.

He shrugged his shoulders.

'Perhaps. But the circumstances now are different. Italy cannot help you. Countries which at the time of our collapse were stunned into a state of stupor are awakening. Let us continue to be frank, Herr Baron. Hitler cannot afford to risk a revolution in France. I can start one.'

'Can you give me evidence of that?'

'If you had no reason to believe it there would be no purpose in coming here,' he said, and that, of course, was true. My coming and my keeping of the terms of his agreement proved my anxiety.

I lifted my left hand.

'Right, Herr Mondel! I will accept your premise. You can discuss the matter with me on terms equal to those of a leader of a free country. But there is one thing which must be fully understood; you must have no association with the Committee of Free France, or with the British.'

'I shall decide one way or the other,' declared Mondel. 'I have received an offer of support from London. I alone have to decide who can best be relied on to help rebuild France.'

For the first time I was close to losing my temper, but still I controlled myself.

'M'sieu Mondel, you forget that there is no way in which the British can render you assistance.'

'Direct assistance,' he reminded me in that gentle voice. He was smiling a little. 'The decision will depend on the amount of indirect help possible, Herr Baron. I will put the situation crudely. Will I receive more help from Germany because I rely on Germany to maintain its promises owing to its new difficulties, or shall I be wiser to accept the indirect help of the British, who will keep their promises and will not promise more than they can achieve? There is a risk either way; my difficulty is to choose the lesser.'

I said thickly: 'You will be wise not to take this line tomorrow.'

'I have not yet decided whether to attend tomorrow's meeting,' said Mondel calmly, 'but I can give you this assurance, Baron. If I do attend it, I shall have already decided to take the risk of relying on the co-operation of Germany. You are a hard-headed and practical man with whom I can talk freely. Now you know my attitude. I can-

177

not make it clearer. You will see the need for finding out what attitude there is at Berchtesgarten, and advising me. When you are ready to advise me, I will send instructions where we can meet. It will not be here.'

The man was acting as if I were a junior officer! I wondered if his visions of power in France had not turned his head. But still I kept my temper: I think Elsa's hand pressing gently on my shoulder made that easier.

'You forgot, m'sieu, that the meeting with the Leader is for tomorrow at two o'clock.'

'I can be ready,' said Mondel. 'If it is too soon for you it can be postponed.'

'Postponed!' I said the word as a man in a daze, and then I roared: 'Postponed! Do you imagine that the Führer will be ready to alter his arrangements for you? Are you aware that he has already come to France to see you? Because it is for the betterment of both countries it is likely that he will agree to reasonable conditions . . .'

'I have a set of the conditions here,' said Mondel, taking a sealed envelope from his pocket. I was aware of Elsa and Joachim staring at him; and of his daughter, who had returned to the foot of the stairs and was also watching tensely. I was like a man in a dream. Did this man imagine he could dictate any terms?

I snatched the envelope. Joachim leaned over my shoulder and broke the seal for me. I unfolded the typewritten papers, and read them slowly. I need not reproduce them all, but four clauses I can remember word for word. A characteristic of the conditions was their clearness and precision.

Clause 2.
All civil services including police, customs, local Government and Central Government will be confined to French people and without influence or coercion from Germany.

Clause 5.
No arms or armament work including that of repair will be undertaken by France for Germany.

178

Clause 7.
 France will maintain an Army sufficient to ensure the security of new frontiers which are to be determined.

Clause 8.
 No food or clothing or essentials are to be exported to Germany unless in the opinion of the French Government they are surplus to French needs.

Need I write more?

I looked up, fighting against the loss of self-control which threatened, but before I could speak Mondel said quietly:

'You were given a demonstration of the strength of the revolutionaries in Vichy, Herr Baron. Neither before nor after the signing of Peace Terms, which these embody in the essentials, will the strength of the independent forces be weakened. The only way in which to enforce rejection of these terms is by further military action in unoccupied France. If your Government decides that such a step is justified'—he shrugged his shoulders—'France will again be the theatre of war. The British are ready and *I can let them in.*'

No man—I say again, *no* man—could have made any intelligent answer to such statements, to such conditions, in the space of the few minutes at my disposal. I was sick with a realisation that Mondel was right, and that the Reich could not afford to reopen hostilities with France. My earlier thought of a complete purge of Vichy was but a dream. In my heart I knew that a new Armistice and even Peace Terms on these conditions would have to be signed. I knew that as if the assurance came from the mouth of the Leader himself. Any further crushing of France, the complete subjection which I had imagined already in being, would have to come after Britain was conquered. The British were ready, he had said. That meant he had been in constant touch with them—oh, I believed him. He had probably negotiated through Murdoch, which would explain why Murdoch and Mondel had worked together and yet independently of each other.

It explained also why Murdoch had lost trace of Mondel.

Mondel was fighting for *France*. Murdoch and the British would not want him to discuss any terms with the Reich, no matter how favourable to France; they wanted his active support. And he had disappeared, evading Murdoch as well as von Stroem, while he made up his mind. This simple, homely man had such cunning! .

I said: 'What guarantee have I that you will not co-operate with enemy nations even if this agreement is made?'

'The guarantee that I want peace in my country!' flashed Mondel. 'I will co-operate with the British only if it is obvious that your Government plans to sabotage the agreecent once it is signed.'

'*Yes,*' said a voice from the window. '*I was afraid of that.*'

A voice from the window. It broke across Mondel's words, and my thoughts. It made Elsa gasp, and Joachim stiffen. It made the young woman by the stairs catch her breath and raise her hands to her breast. It had on me an effect more shattering than any high explosive, *because it was Murdoch's voice.*

I stared at the window.

At first I saw no one, and then a shadow loomed, and after it the head and shoulders of a man. Behind him were two others, Fuller and Angell; they made a show of automatics which meant that physically they had control of the situation. There was worse to come. Behind the first man, I say, were Fuller and Angell; and the first man was surely Murdoch.

It was not.

I was looking at the face of von Stroem, and I believed it was von Stroem before *Murdoch's voice* came from his lips, mocking and derisive, very confident.

'A shock, Baron? Too bad. Someone forgot to tell you that von Stroem *and* his man Lirchner died in a car accident three months ago. I didn't put up a bad show, did I?'

As he spoke he put a leg over the low window sill, and climbed in.

27

Could it be True?

Could it be true?

It was impossible to believe, even with the evidence of his voice. Only that was in any way reminiscent of Murdoch. For the rest it was von Stroem, with the bloodshot eyes in which the tiny veins stood out, with the dark, close-cropped hair, dark brows and lashes, the dissipated face—the face, I had thought when I had first seen him—of a man who was living too fast. The square lips, the square jaw without a cleft, even the sloping forehead.

Only the voice was Murdoch's.

Yet I had seen Murdoch as himself at *l'Hôtel Grande,* I had even seen the mole on his cheek, a little more than an hour after I had seen von Stroem. No disguise *could* be so effective and yet removed so swiftly and also re-applied. With plastic surgery I could have understood it, but this . . .

'Oh yes, it is I,' said Murdoch. 'Good afternoon, m'sieu,' he added to Mondel, who I believe was almost as stupefied as I. 'The explanation's a simple one, Baron—the injection of paraffin wax by the newest method—all done in half-an hour, although not painless. The real trouble is the eyes —I didn't like the injections to make them bloodshot one little bit, but it had to be a good job. Eh, Elsa?'

Elsa was breathing very hard.

It was Mondel who broke the silence, one which I could not have interrupted, for it was physically impossible for me to speak. My throat was so constricted that it was most difficult to breath; my neck was swelling, my lungs felt like bursting.

As from a long way off I heard Mondel say:]

'Murdoch—what is this?'

'Well,' replied Murdoch with the air of a man who has a most unpleasant duty, 'it is like this, m'sieu. My instructions were to try to get Vichy into a state bordering on revolution but to keep it bordering until you were ready to co-operate. But you hardly played fair, did you? While you negotiated with us you treated with the Boche as well. Has nothing persuaded you that even if they wanted to be sincere it would be a physical impossibility? Or mental? Or spiritual? Take your choice.'

'I still do not understand,' Mondel said stiffly. 'I have made it clear that my one concern is to remove the existing stranglehold on France, and I shall do that whichever way I think best.'

'Oh, no,' said Murdoch.

'I shall . . .'

'Oh, no,' repeated Murdoch. 'You will join us, or you'll do nothing. Rather than have a fresh President and fresh Armistice terms—call 'em Peace, if you like—working with so-called co-operation with Germany, we shall stick to the old gang. We do know what we're up against with them.'

'Are you suggesting . . .' Mondel's voice rose.

'You are fated to be interrupted, aren't you?' asked Murdoch. 'I am suggesting that we cannot allow you to come to terms with Germany. So we are taking you to England, where General de Gaulle will have much to say to you.'

'England!' exclaimed Mondel.

'A pleasant country,' said Murdoch. 'Far better even under bombing than Paris is under Hitler. You know, M'sieu Mondel, you have very nearly double-crossed us, as I was afraid you would. It is as well I was von Stroem *and* myself, wasn't it? Otherwise I would have had no idea how serious you were about your negotiations with Hitler. They were necessary, you told me as Murdoch, to complete the arrangements amongst the people. So as Murdoch I encouraged them. But as von Stroem I didn't at all like the way you were moving. And when you disappeared I was really worried.'

He paused. I had to let him talk, for there was nothing I could do or say: I was fighting too hard for my breath. I could see no way out of this, no way of stopping Murdoch from taking Mondel away.

'The trouble is,' went on Murdoch, 'that it's such a long story, even though this is the end. von Horssell, you know the situation as well as I. With Mondel's co-operation I can make the country rise up, without it there will be localised risings which your murderers will crush with bloody purges. I won't risk that if I can help it. And when I say "I", read "we". I am acting under direct orders to get M'sieu Mondel's help or leave things as they are. After this I can't trust Mondel, so I am leaving things as they are. But remember this, you butcher. We shall come through France when we are ready, and the people will be waiting for us.'

'You are talking madness,' said Mondel softly. 'I have slowly attained control of the country, my influence is so great that my disappearance will do more harm to the Allied cause than anything since Dakar.'

'Wrong in one,' said Murdoch promptly. 'Officially, you will have escaped *voluntarily* to England. You will leave a message with all your editors to print that fact, and de Gaulle will broadcast that you have decided the moment for rising is not yet. You will be quite a hero, m'sieu, the French will admire you tremendously. And incidentally, wrong in two. We—including de Gaulle's people and mine —have subsidised your influence, you could never have reached the point you have without us. The considerable Free French reaction in France believes you are really with them, and this new development will prove it.'

As an enemy, he was right, of course. And his Government was right. It was wise to wait for the revolution until such time as the position of Germany was even more difficult, if that day should come. In my state of mind as I listened it was almost possible to believe that Germany could lose. A traitorous thought, perhaps; I simply record it as my feelings then.

But I could not speak—it was physically impossible. I could think, however, and my thoughts were deadly. I rejoiced in one thing only: that his woman was dead. He must have known it, by now, since as von Stroem he had pretended to accept the news with delight.

It was the only brightness in the shadows about me.

Mondel seemed to have shrunken within himself. His daughter was all eyes—I remember that they were a deep blue, the exact shade of Mary Dell's.

It was Elsa who spoke.

It was good to hear her voice sounding normal as it did —clearly she had recovered from the shock of the discovery.

'Murdoch, why did you come for us?'

He looked at her with his bloodshot eyes which could not laugh as Murdoch's laughed, although there was the mocking note in his voice that I knew and hated.

'When you look back carefully you will realise that the purges and the cruelties which von Stroem inspired ceased three months ago—executions were postponed through lack of evidence, a dozen things were altered. I even put up a mild man for the Chief of Police in Vienna. But I had to live as von Stroem, a man particularly fitted to be impersonated—a man of mystery who rarely visited Berchtesgarten, who kept himself very much to himself, with only his three personal bodyguards. They included Lirchner. Two of the bodyguards he killed himself, before I got him with Lirchner. There was no one alive who could easily identify him, *except his mistress*.'

I drew a sharp breath, and it cleared my vocal cords, so that I uttered the words which sprang to my mind.

'You mean Mitzi Weiner?'

'I mean Mitzi,' said Murdoch gently. 'And I learned that Mitzi remained with him because he guaranteed the safety of her parents. No small sacrifice even for parents, but the race you dislike so much, von Horssell, is capable of great sacrifices. So I saw her, and explained; and she helped me. I might even say that without her I could not have succeeded, for the rumour that von Stroem had a Jewish mistress was widespread, even if it had not reached you. More people knew Mitzi than knew von Stroem by sight. You will be sorry to know that she is now in England; I arranged for her and family to fly there yesterday.'

'One day I will see that she suffers,' I grated.

Murdoch eyed me curiously.

'You still don't realise what has happened to you,' he said, with a hardening in his voice. 'I might have left you, you're a washed-out old invalid, anyhow. But that trick with Mary can't be forgiven.'

I licked my lips.

'Frightened?' he mocked me.

I was not frightened and I think he must have known it. I had only one concern—the cause of the Reich—and while I lived I could further it.

Elsa answered for me.

'You know that is impossible,' she said. 'But Murdoch—it is an incomparabe feat! The disguise alone—the impersonation—it does not seem credible. But you have not answered my question: why did you send for us?'

'So you haven't seen that, Elsa? Poor, poor Fräulein, your mind is getting as stultified as the Baron's, I should try some of his precious serum. The truth of the situation in Vichy was leaking through to Berchtesgarten. I discovered through Mary, who has been in Vienna for six months, that they were thinking of using you again. The skeleton of your organisation remained—Schlesser in Paris, Voss, and a dozen others, would gladly work for you. Directly I heard the rumour I went to Berchtesgarten. I had not been there—as von Stroem—for a year. I have rarely seen any of the officials. I had some bad moments, but I got through, and again Mitzi was the key. They knew of her, and I allowed it to be known that she was in Vienna with me. So—*I* advised asking your help. It was already in their minds, they thought that I was falling into their trap. But they didn't know that I was proposing to get you on the run from the start. You haven't had time to think clearly, not even the great Baron von Horssell!'

That *was* true; and Elsa gave a reluctant nod.

'And things in France were coming to a head,' Murdoch continued. 'Once Hitler arrived for the meeting with Mondel, which was *not* arranged through von Stroem but privately, although I came to hear of it—things would move one way or the other. Berchtesgarten would decide on a full-weight attack, or an agreement with Mondel. So von Stroem's number was up, and I could take chances. I needn't go over it again. Mondel is coming with us to England. I think things will go on as they are when the need for a further purge is gone.'

'How do you propose to get away?' asked Elsa.

'By 'plane, Fraulein.' He mocked us. 'I'm expecting it any time. There is a flat field near here which serves, and the land was surveyed out when I discovered where Mondel was—or when Angell did, he followed a messenger from *Le Noir*. Anything else on your mind, my sweet?' he demanded of Elsa.

'No,' she said.

I cleared my throat, and Murdoch looked towards me. Fuller had also climbed into the window and was at Mondel's side, although I did not think Mondel was capable of thinking clearly, the result of this meeting was such a great shock.

'You were going to say something?' Murdoch inquired.

I said: 'Just this, Murdoch. You may escape, you may take Mondel, you may kill Elsa and Joachim and me—*ach*, we are but small things in the new world which is being built. But you will fail, your country cannot continue the fight much longer. France will be subdued, her factories will work for us, those of all the occupied countries will do the same.'

'I don't think so,' replied Murdoch. 'They are being prepared to bite the dog that bit 'em. For "dog" read "cur", if you prefer. The trouble with mad dogs is that when they bite they cause rabies, and the rabies which is in Europe now is going to kill off quite a lot of Nazis.' He spoke very mildly, but that did not deceive me. 'However, I shall get rid of you here, von Horssell. But before you go, a little piece of information. When you told me as von Stroem what you had done with Mary and then sent me away— you were double-crossing von Stroem nicely—I telephoned the others. Mary was treated with a stomach pump, and they got the tablet out before the coating dissolved. I sent her to England with Mitzi and Mitzi's parents.'

I could only gape at him.

I saw him raise his gun, and believed he would kill me —as I would have killed him. I did not think there was a chance of living; I do not think I cared.

But then Angell spoke from the window, his voice both sharp and urgent.

'Bruce, breakers ahead. There's a mob on the move from a dozen places.'

Murdoch did not look round, but I saw him stiffen.

'How many?' he snapped.

186

'Two hundred, with others to come,' answered Elsa from my side, and there was a note of triumph in her voice. 'You didn't know, did you, that Voss and Brunning were waiting with a strong force to come if there was difficulty here. I had to go outside and give a signal within fifteen minutes of arriving, or they were to advance. How soon will your aeroplane arrive, Murdoch? Just too late to be of use? I shouldn't use that gun, it will make them hurry.'

She stepped forward a little, looking at him with deep satisfaction. Mondel drew in a deep breath, and Joachim smiled—yes, I saw the wide smile of relief on his face.

Murdoch would not get away.

Mondel would remain, Mondel would come to terms —*ach*, now they would probably be altered because he would know he no longer had the support of the British and the Free French, they would not trust him. In the twinkling of an eye the situation had altered, and Murdoch was defeated.

Thanks to Elsa.

'They're coming from all sides, Murdoch,' she said. 'The place is surrounded.'

28

I Report

Elsa was standing at my left side and I put my arm about her and drew her close from sheer exuberance of spirit. I knew that the one chance they had of escape was that the aeroplane would come within the next five minutes, and there was little likelihood of that. Even if it did arrive, Voss and Brunning would bring it down, although it might be allowed to take off.

How I laughed!

Murdoch did not waste time in talking or shooting. He left Fuller in the room with a word of instruction to watch us, and followed Angell through the window.

I could see the fields beyond through the gap which the path made in the ring of trees. I saw at least a dozen men on motor-cycles coming towards the house, and behind them others on foot. The sun glistened on their rifles and bayonets—they were fully prepared for hand-to-hand fighting.

Murdoch's voice was audible, and then that of a man I knew who was to him what Joachim was to me, a paltry Cockney whose manner is at all times impertinent: his name is Briggs—Percival Briggs.

'Blimey!' I heard Briggs say. 'That's a 'ot one, that is.'

'You'll get hot if you don't get a move on,' replied Murdoch. 'Is everything ready?'

'Only gotta give the order,' said Briggs.

'Let them get within fifty yards,' said Murdoch.

The words forced themselves into my mind. They were confidently uttered, and sounded as if Murdoch actually had some plan by which he expected to maintain his safety! *Let them get within fifty yards!*

I saw Elsa's colour fade, while Fuller said with a light voice and as if he were disinterested:

'You never did give Bruce his due, Baron.'

'What is it?' snapped Elsa.

'Eight machine-gun nests are surrounding the house, manned by the faithful Vichy—mostly the guards who let you through when I saw you the other day.'

Eight machine-guns against two hundred men. *Gott in himmel!* I fumed, why had not Voss and Brunning arranged for a thousand men, for armoured cars, for field guns?

Murdoch appeared for a moment at the window.

'Bring Mondel,' he ordered briefly, covering us with his automatic while Fuller obeyed. Mondel made no effort to resist; he was like a man in a stupor, he would have never made the leader he had dreamed of. His daughter said in a low-pitched voice:

'Messieurs, I ...'

'We've room for you, mam'selle,' said Murdoch, and I thought even then that there was a touch of sympathy in his voice. 'But, please, no tricks—it's a hot enough spot as it is.'

'Can you escape?' she asked.

'If we can hold them off for twenty minutes, yes.'

Twenty minutes! He needed as much time as that before his aeroplane arrived. If there had been some way in which we could have warned Brunning and Voss! Had they kept their distance and started their attack when the aeroplane landed, then it would put finish to Murdoch's hopes.

Murdoch was replaced by an unshaven Frenchman as he hurried away. I could hear the staccato mutter of the motor-cycles getting much nearer, and I waited in dread of the opening bark of the machine-guns. It was Elsa who took a half-step forward, while Joachim followed her example and protected me from the man at the window.

'M'sieu, it will be impossible for you to get away,' Elsa said in her fluent French. 'Thousands of men are coming to support the advance guard. For your help we will pay you a thousand francs.'

'Two thousand!' I barked.

'If you will please make it a million,' replied the Frenchman with a swift smile, 'I will not spit at you.'

While Elsa was gripping my hand and while I knew that Joachim was reckoning the chances of getting at his gun, the guard deliberately spat, so that the spittle hit the floor near Elsa's feet.

'German bitch,' he said, 'remember I am more accurate with the gun.'

If there was any attempt on Joachim's part or Elsa's, he would shoot. There was nothing we could do but stay there, our ears filled with the ever-increasing sound of the motor-cycles. There was no doubt they were no more than two hundred yards away. Some two miles beyond them, on flat country, the infantry were advancing.

Fifty yards.

Twenty!

I judged that was the distance when the machine-guns opened fire. The bark of them came from all sides of the house, and I knew that Murdoch had not lied. I saw three motor-cyclists fall from their machines, which careered crazily about the fields before crashing. But two cyclists were not hit, and they carried sub-machine guns. They opened fire, and there was bedlam in and around the house. Bullets even spattered against the window of the room I was

189

in, and suddenly I heard a gasp from the guard; *and he fell backwards.*

Fate had thrown a chance into our hands!

Joachim went forward very swiftly to the window. Elsa turned and I saw her straining at a heavy settee which she dragged across the door, to make sure that it could not easily be opened. Joachim went through the window and Elsa stayed by it, keeping to one side, and with an automatic in her hand with which to shoot anyone who came near.

I heard the sharper note of Joachim's gun.

I also thought that there was an immediate lessening in the degree of the shooting from Murdoch's men. I knew a great hope, that Joachim would put some of the machine-gunners out of action. I was hardly aware of the danger as I peered through the window.

The two cyclists who had broken through fell from their machines. The shooting continued, then stopped abruptly. Perhaps fifteen minutes remained of the time Murdoch said he required, and the infantry were a mile and three-quarters away.

Time had never passed so slowly.

There was silence about me, and I was unaware even of the fact that when Murdoch returned to shoot me and Elsa he would find what he had not expected. I did not want to see him. I prayed only that the infantry should arrive before the aeroplane. I knew that if there was any sense at all in Brunning or in Voss they would by now have sent for reinforcements. Armoured cars must surely come soon.

When five minutes remained, I saw Joachim. He was limping badly, but reached the window and, with a great effort, managed to climb through it. He dragged a chair and dropped into it so that he could shoot anyone who attacked.

Soon, I heard the drone of the aeroplane. Time began to fly. I saw the machine circling about the house as it prepared to land. I hoped that it would land near the front, so that we could shoot when Murdoch and the others ran for it, but it landed out of sight. I heard footsteps and the mutter of voices. The engines of the 'plane did not stop.

There was no shooting, even from our advancing forces; they were too far away for accuracy.

The French machine-gunners moved off; they were mobile units, and would escape to breed more treachery.

I had one hope left, that Murdoch would come to carry out his threat, that he could be stopped from escaping alive. But he did not rate my death high enough to risk his own. In that decision he showed great contempt for me and my power.

He did not fear me: and thus he robbed me of much of my moral strength.

Suddenly I heard the engines of the aeroplane quicken, and their drone deepen. A few seconds later I saw it flying off. I could see the heads of the occupants of the cabin but could distinguish no individual. I heard bursts of shooting, but they were ineffective.

The aeroplane dwindled to a black spot against the sky, and disappeared.

. . . . .

I reported all of this to Berchtesgarten by telephone, and the visit of the Leader to Vichy was, of course, postponed. You will know of the fact that France continued in a state of semi-rebellion; a general rising was feared too much. Yes, feared by the Reich! I was received later by the Leader himself, and he was most gracious to me, understanding the difficulties against which I had worked. I made it clear to him that I tried to kill Mondel since he had planned a general rising.

I know that much of Mondel's influence remains.

The Free French radio is constantly telling the French that de Gaulle and Mondel and others are preparing for the day of revolution and of victory, and although I am now in charge of unoccupied France, it is impossible—and unwise—to prevent the radio news being received. France is riddled with spies, I am at times afraid of what might happen.

But slowly, remorselessly, I work to prevent it. If the British set foot again in France it will not be easy for them to take the country in order to attack the Reich But day in and day out the shadow of such a possibility haunts me.

I work on, with Elsa, Voss and Brunning—it was madness to have believed anything between those two, Elsa had finally convinced me of that. Yet I cannot but wonder, sometimes, if she is faithful to me. She is often with Voss; is it always on business?

Joachim recovered well, and serves me with the faithfulness which is part of him. With Elsa he is always thoughtful and considerate, and they act on my instructions so well that I am frequently moved to congratulate them—and Voss, for that matter.

The other thing: I learned that Mary Dell had fully recovered. I wished with all that is in me that I could have heard differently; such are the contradictions in the mind of man.

Sometimes I talk of Murdoch's impersonation with Elsa, and recall the little indications that should have alerted us. One above all others was the wound in his cheek. It was clear of course that Brunning had *not* hit him. But he needed a wound, since I had caused a minor one with my stick, and so he had actually allowed himself to be shot, showing me the bullet score.

Yes, he is a very clever man.

I have since learned that he planned, if Mondel had decided to work with him, to stage the uprising in Vichy to coincide with the Leader's arrival in the city. That indignity and outrage I prevented. It is some consolation to know that, some easing of my bitterness against Murdoch and Dell.

Often I wonder when I shall meet them again; the day will surely come.